I0741745

Roadkill on the Flipside

A NOVEL

Dean Ammerman

KABLOONA

Eagan, Minnesota

Library of Congress Control Number: 2017910225

ISBN: 978-0-9846822-6-3

August 2017

KABLOONA

"In the ashes we are all leveled."

—SENECA (THE YOUNGER)

Roadkill on the Flipside

1

No Solicitors

I was fighting a cold or the flu. And losing.

I lay huddled beneath a musty old quilt on our living room couch wearing my Power Rangers boxers and faded yellow T-shirt, and watching infomercials on TV. My nose was running, my head was pounding, my glands were swollen and I'm pretty sure I had a temperature of at least 162 degrees. Maybe more.

Which is when I heard a loud knock on the front door.

Actually, it was more demolition than knock. You see, a foot-long axe blade reduced our 100-year-old oak door to splinters, even though we had a perfectly good doorbell and a sign that said "No Solicitors."

"Nobody's home," I said, diving deep within the questionable security of the quilt.

Loud footsteps. A screeching cat. A broken table. A smashed television. A grunt.

Silence.

I peeked out from underneath the cover and rubbed my puffy, bloodshot eyes. Standing directly above me was an old and flabby one-armed soldier dressed in worn brown leather armor. A dull red burn scar disfigured half of his face and an out-of-control beard, bent nose and leather helmet obscured the other half.

"Upstairs," I said through several layers of phlegm and a coughing fit. I pointed vaguely in the direction of the stairs and up.

The soldier snarled, peeled the quilt off my body and poked the razor-sharp edge of the axe into my sternum.

"You Delgado?" he said.

"Maybe," I squeaked, trying hard not to faint or bleed.

The truth was (and is), I *am* Wilkin Delgado, even if I don't always like to admit it. I'm sixteen years old and I live in a small Minnesota town called Warrensberg, which is in the exact center of the universe. Normally my life is pretty boring, but about once a year an intergalactic plumber named Cardamon Webb comes to my house and asks for help—to fix a nasty sewage problem (as an example) or figure out how to turn on the fresh water from the Source (as another example) or find a missing Ma-Loo somewhere in the infinite expanding universe (as a last example). My friends Cassandra Filipi and Rob Cho think those are lame excuses and that I'm just skipping school for the fun of it. They also think I'm "certifiable" because I once mentioned something about being attacked by a Gutrog and another time I told them about the Key to the City of the Dead, which I always wear on a leather cord around my neck. Knowing all that, you can understand why I wasn't exactly alarmed when that overweight alien soldier with one arm crashed through our front door and threatened me with a dangerous weapon.

"I got instructions," he said.

"Leave them on the table next to the Kleenex box," I said politely. "And close what's left of the door on your way out." At the end I even added a friendly "Please."

4

He growled and leaned down so his face was inches away from my own. Even through my clogged sinuses I could tell he smelled like a wet ostrich, which is not a good thing.

"This is serious, son," he said. "We're at war."

"Like I said, Alice Jane is upstairs." I pointed again. "She likes to fight."

As you might have guessed, I was referring to Alice Jane Zelinski, who is probably the closest thing Warrensberg has to a warrior, since she's always walking around with an eight-foot-long Iknatian spear and also carries a smelly pink Birkin purse that she uses to clobber people like me over the head whenever she feels like it. And she takes Kung Fu lessons, too. Alice Jane is seventeen years old and originally from Kansas City, Missouri, where she was the three-time tug-o-war champion of something or other. (I forget what.) She also has spiky gray hair, sharp elbows and smells like bacon. Plus, after being carbonized, she now has weird fractal shapes swimming around inside her body like a flesh-and-blood aquarium. It's creepy.

"Who?" the soldier asked.

One more thing. Alice Jane is rich. Seriously rich. In fact, she owns practically the entire universe, except for about two trecentillion Slurbish rodondos. Last year she got everything everywhere legally registered in her name through an amazing superhuman feat of negotiation and butt-saving. After that, everybody kind of expected (and hoped!) she'd leave town and move to some ritzy fashion planet a million light years away. But because of a second restraining order and the fact that she's now under house arrest, Alice Jane is stuck in Warrensberg, living in our big old house with her mom (Fake Aunt Marie), her cat (Genghis), my mom (Mrs. Delgado), me and two Metazoan Nards (Alex and Nardzilla). She also has a huge satellite antenna on the roof and about 3,000 pairs of fancy, expensive shoes that are piled sky-high in just about every corner of the house.

"Alice Jane Zelinski," I said. "That's who you want."

"I'm here for *you*, Delgado," the soldier said.

Huh?

"I'm no warrior," I said.

"Give me a few days and you will be," he said.

"Who are you?" I asked.

I didn't like his manners. Or the sharp edge of his axe. Or the ostrich smell.

"Grimes," he said.

"What do you want with me, Mr. Grimes?"

I coughed and blew my nose.

"Supposed to bring you back to fight in the war. You're some kind of 'Secret Weapon' is what he tells me."

When Grimes said all that, my fever-addled mind raced through four brief but critical questions: Fight? War? Secret Weapon? He? Plus one free bonus question: Why would anybody want me to fight in a far away deadly place knowing that I occasionally have trouble remembering to wear socks?

"I'm sick," I finally said, gently pushing the axe aside and pulling the quilt back up to my neck.

"I can bring your corpse, if you'd prefer," he said. "Webb didn't say anything about needing you alive."

"Webb? As in *Cardamon* Webb?" I asked.

"Said you might be uncooperative," Grimes said.

I was confused. I mean, whenever Cardamon Webb needed my help, he came in person or sent Loretta the puffin. And his requests always had to do with a major plumbing problem, not fighting or wars.

"Can I see those instructions of yours?" I asked.

Grimes dug his only hand into the leather breastplate of his armor and pulled out a piece of paper covered with Cardamon Webb's familiar loopy handwriting. The note was beat-up and smudged and hard to read.

"'Please accompany Mr. Delgado to Eris,'" I read aloud. "'Try to avoid....'" I stopped reading, scrunched my face and asked Grimes, "What's *this* word?"

"I think it's 'dismemberment,'" he said, squinting at the page. "Which is why I didn't dismember you."

"Thanks," I said.

He grunted.

"'Try to avoid dismemberment at all costs,'" I finished. It was signed "C.W."

As I struggled to untangle the meaning of the plumber's words, I heard a crash and a loud "Blerk!" coming from the room directly above us.

Grimes looked up and then at me.

I blew my nose again.

Seconds later, Alice Jane Zelinski came storming down the stairs dressed in a neon pink yoga outfit, a pair of fuzzy sheepskin slippers and a gray electronic tracking monitor around her left ankle. She was in one of her surly moods, as you might expect.

"Everything is down!" she screeched, brandishing the Iknatian spear in her right hand. "The markets. My contracts and financials. *And* my Alexander Wang Kori Chelsea Boot order. I'm totally locked out!"

"Um," I said, looking at Alice Jane and gesturing toward the dumpy alien soldier beside me.

"Who's the freak?" she asked me, eyeing the old man and glancing at the broken door, table and TV. She took a step forward and poked the spear threateningly at the soldier's bulging midsection.

"Grimes," I said.

"*Sergeant* Grimes," he said, gently setting his axe on the fractured coffee table.

"You the one that screwed up my network?" Alice Jane roared.

"I'm here for Delgado," Grimes said gruffly. "To fight in the war."

"Dodobrain?" she said incredulously.

I nodded.

"Good luck with that," she said, lowering the spear.

I didn't appreciate the lack of support, even if I did agree with her.

"Cardamon Webb sent him," I said to Alice Jane.

I handed her the message.

"What's this word?" she asked, pointing at the middle of the page.

"'Dismemberment,'" Grimes and I said at the same time.

Alice Jane nodded, returned the note, turned and walked back up the stairs.

"Have fun, Wilkin," she said. "And try not to screw things up this time."

2

In Denial

Access Denied.

That's what the screen on every one of my twenty-four monitors, five tablets and sixteen phones said as I attempted to connect to the PT Interstellar Communication Network from my bedroom office command center. I tried rebooting. (No luck.) Then I contacted Customer Support. ("Your call is very important to us. Your wait time is five … weeks … and … three … days … and … fourteen … hours … and … eleven … minutes.") Next I smashed a window. (I felt a lot better.) And finally I screamed. ("Blerk!") None of that helped, so I grabbed my spear, kicked open the door and stomped downstairs to see if I could locate (and possibly skewer) the source of the problem, which was probably Wilkin Delgado.

In case you're clueless about me and my living situation, my name is Alice Jane Zelinski LLC. (I'm now a Limited Liability Corporation.) My mom, my cat and I share a two-story crap house in Dorkville, Minnesota, with Wilkin, his mom and two…others. I've been staying in this garbage dump for like three years, ever since the "disturbing violent episode" (as my first psycho doctor described it) back in Kansas City when I broke seven bones in Jeremy Lynn Mansfield's wimpy right hand. (He deserved it.) So naturally I was exiled to godforsaken Minnesota to hide out and keep a low profile, which isn't all that easy when you're an übersexy gorgeous figure of womanly perfection like I am.

After that it got complicated.

As unbelievable as it sounds, there's this flip-flop-wearing plumber from outer space who came to Warrensberg and somehow convinced Wilkin and me to help him save the universe three times. Which we did. (You're welcome.) Along the way I got my earlobes blown off, my butt branded with the "Royal P" logo and my entire body carbonized so I'm like some kind of living lava lamp.

The upside? I now own pretty much everything in the universe and employ nearly four million lawyers and a team of virtual administrative assistants that are all named Ned. And I run the cosmos from the privacy of my bedroom.

I'd like to relocate back to Kansas City, but right now I'm stuck in Dorkville because of two restraining orders (one in Missouri and the other in Minnesota) and a slight misunderstanding with a half-dozen narrow-minded government officials and one stubborn Warrensberg police officer by the name of Dennis.

I get it. Most people don't like to be kicked, punched or strangled. (Even for a good cause.) My social worker Carol reminds me of that every time she visits the house to check on my "progress" and oversee my 10,000 hours of court-ordered community service. "You're helping others and making the world a better place, Miss Zelinski," Carol tells me. Yeah, right. That's what got me in trouble in the first place.

It's like this. I have these two friends who happen to be

Zorazeens from the Lombo-Geebo nebula, and like any out-of-towners they look a little bit different [like grungy manatees wearing fedora hats and pink "I (heart) Warrensberg" T-shirts], which scares some folks, if you can believe that. So when Ceek and Wergo (as they call themselves) moved into the neighborhood a few doors away, Mrs. Shirley Itasco from down the block put up a stink and went all the way to the City Council to get them evicted and deported along with their 413 kids who consider me their godmother.

With me so far?

Like any upstanding good citizen I went to the City Council meeting and got involved in the democratic process. That's when I accidentally threatened our esteemed elected officials and inadvertently took part in a brief interactive presentation that the *Warrensberg Watchtower* called "a full-scale riot." All I was trying to do was enlighten the six Council members, half of the police force, Mrs. Itasco and the rest of the town about the peaceful and misunderstood Zorazeens. It was a mission of mercy, pure and simple.

As of right now, Ceek and Wergo are "provisionally" allowed to live in their townhome, and Wergo can continue to drive a school bus for the district. Me? I was ordered to stay away from the entire Council, the Chief of Police (Dennis) and Mrs. Itasco, and sentenced to 10,000 hours of supervised community service. Worst of all, I have to wear an ugly tracking monitor on my left ankle, since I'm also under house arrest for "an unspecified period of time or until Miss Zelinski chooses to leave the country, the sooner the better," as the judge told me and my lawyers in court.

That was months ago. And I'm over it. Almost.

Which gets me back to "Access denied" and the fact that I couldn't do any work or order any super cute outfits like I wanted to do because I was locked out of my network. So I went down the stairs ready to chew out Wilkin, only to find him on the couch in his underwear talking to some fatty Spartacus wannabe with one arm and a big hatchet in his hand.

"Which of you wants to die?" I said nicely. I mean, the connection to all my holdings and employees and planets and finances was totally shut down. I was pissed. Can you blame me?

Scaredy-cat Wilkin ratted out the stranger (of course), who dropped his weapon after I pointed the spear tip in the direction of his unprotected liver.

"None of my devices can get onto the network," I explained, "and you two are the only ones in the house who might have caused the problem."

Actually, Alex and Nardzilla could have been responsible, but I was pretty sure they were still asleep or shedding their leaves or whatever Metazoan Nards do in their spare time. Besides, these days Nardzilla was more interested in her boyfriend Carl than causing any kind of trouble.

"I'm here for Delgado," the man said.

Seriously?

"Cardamon Webb sent him," Wilkin said, handing me a piece of paper. "His name is Grimes. He wants me to fight in a war."

"Good luck with that," I said after reading the note.

It was good news. The two of them were headed off to a far away war that didn't involve me, which meant I could spread out and use Wilkin's room to store my new collection of designer handbags. So I went back to my office, closed the door and let out a peaceful sigh. That didn't last long, though. "Access denied" stared back at me from every corner of the room.

Now what?

My next thought was that the login issue could be a problem with the network itself, so I called up my best friend Leo in Kansas

City. Leo is like my only real human friend in the universe. Before I relocated to Dorkville he even tattooed an eyeball on the back of my neck that I can actually see out of. (Which he still doesn't believe.)

"Leo, I can't access the network on any of my devices," I told him.

"Hold on," he said.

Leo is a computer genius. He also does art and he's a hacker, too. Last year when I got all that money and power, I told him he could order whatever he wanted as long as he'd do a little freelance troubleshooting for me. He went ahead and built this crazy cyber electronic sanctum sanctorum in his parents' basement where he can connect with just about any civilized world in the universe. It's paid off, too. When I was having trouble with an uncooperative planet in an obscure outlying galaxy, he hacked into their weather management system. As a result, I can bury them in hail and hurricanes by clicking an app on my phone. Which means I pretty much get whatever I want. (Mostly expensive handbags and shoes.)

"Got it, Alice Jane," Leo said. "But it doesn't look good."

"What's the deal?" I asked.

"You're totally off the grid," Leo said.

"I know that," I said. "The question is: Why?"

"Give me a minute," he said.

In the background I could hear the click-click-click of his fingers on a keyboard and the word "Interesting" and a "Come on, come on" here and there.

"Well?" I said impatiently.

"I think I found the problem," Leo said.

"Can you fix it?"

"Not really," he said slowly. "Alice Jane, according to the latest news reports, you were found dead thirty-seven minutes ago."

13

3

The Flipside

Sigh.

I wanted to stay in Warrensberg and get over my cold (and live a long and happy life, too, if you really want to know), but apparently that wasn't one of my choices. After Alice Jane retreated up the stairs, Grimes lifted me high into the air and threw me to the floor.

"Pack," he said. "Now."

"I'll need to talk to my mom," I said, slowly getting to my feet. "I mean, I'm underage and all, so I think leaving Earth without her permission is against the law."

"It's war," Grimes said. "There are no laws."

That didn't sound good.

"Where exactly are we going?" I asked, stepping away from the irritable soldier.

"FEBA," he said.

"Where's that?"

"Forward Edge of the Battle Area," Grimes said. "The front line."

That sounded even worse.

"Is this FEBA on the Other side or the Underside?" I asked as a point of clarification.

You see, according to Cardamon Webb, the universe is like an Oreo. It has an Outside, an Inside and an Other side, as well as a metaphysical Underside, even though it really has only one side and is infinite like a Möbius strip. And in case that makes sense, the universe is also made up of different Realities stacked like potato crisps in a giant Pringles can. Just thinking about all that made my brain hurt and my mouth salivate.

"Flipside," Grimes said.

In other words, none of the above.

"Um," I began confusedly, "what and where is this 'Flipside'?"

"Look around," he said, turning clockwise in a circle. "It's like everything you see, except turned inside out."

What kind of answer was that?

"So how do we get from here to there?" I asked.

"Flippers," he said.

I nodded a couple of times like I knew what he was talking about, which I didn't.

"I have one more question," I said, even though I had like 113 questions, and questions stacked on top of those questions. "What is this war about? I mean, can't we just sit down and reason with these people, whoever they are?"

"Been going on for more than 2,500 years," Grimes said. "Nobody knows or cares what it's about. We fight."

"Maybe if we talked instead," I said hopefully.

"Pack," he said again, hefting his axe. "Or I'll rethink the 'dismemberment' part."

I went upstairs to my room and put on my jeans and bug pin. I even remembered to wear socks. (A miracle.) Then I tossed a polar fleece, wool hat, sunglasses, toothbrush and extra pair of jeans into my duffle bag. That was pretty much it. I mean, I was already wearing my lucky Power Rangers boxers and the Key to the City of the Dead. What else did I need?

I sat down at my desk and wrote a quick note:

Mom—
Gone to the Flipside to help Cardamon Webb. Not sure when I'll be back.
—Wilkin
P.S. Be sure to water Alex while I'm gone.

After that I went back downstairs. I'd only been gone a few minutes, but in that short amount of time the entire floor was completely trashed. Dust and plaster bits were everywhere, the furniture was in pieces, the carpet was shredded, books had been torn apart, and the dividing wall between the living room and kitchen was a pile of rubble. Grimes leaned casually against the fireplace, enjoying the latest issue of *Good Housekeeping* magazine.

My mom was not going to be happy.

On the plus side, my sinuses had opened up, and all of my mental effort imagining inside-out Oreos seemed to have cured my fever and headache.

I was ready to go.

"Where do we find a Flipper?" I asked, stumbling over the remains of a former ottoman and sidestepping a broken floor lamp.

"This way," Grimes said, grabbing me roughly by the shoulder and pushing me through the open doorway and into the sunlight.

Now you might think the neighbors would be a little curious or even call the police if they saw a strange, one-armed soldier with a big axe dragging a disgruntled sixteen-year-old kid down the sidewalk. Nope. Once the Zorazeens arrived and other weird-looking aliens appeared, everybody except Mrs. Itasco closed their blinds and pretended Warrensberg was the same as it had always been: Boring.

"What can you tell me about soldier training?" I asked. "I'm getting a C-minus in gym is why I ask."

"Not much to it, really," Grimes said, using a piece of our splintered door to dislodge something yellow from between his teeth. "Every new recruit is issued a uniform and a weapon—sword or axe, your choice—and somebody points you toward the enemy."

"What about combat tactics and physical conditioning?"

"Doesn't really matter. Most recruits only last a few days," he said. "And lives are cheap."

Grimes wasn't doing a good job selling the whole "going to war" thing.

"What about you? How long have you been fighting?"

"Since I was your age, I suppose," he said thoughtfully. "Lost my arm in my first battle." Then he touched the scar on the side of his face. "Got the burn a couple years back."

I looked past the armor and the battle scars and into his seen-it-all eyes.

"You're a hero," I said.

"Ordinary soldier is what I am," Grimes said, looking distractedly into the sky and beyond. "We do what we have to do."

"What about me? What's *my* job?"

"Webb says he wants you at the FEBA," Grimes said. Then he took a long, meditative breath and loosened his grip on me a little. "Look, son, you're better off if you don't ask questions. On account of that'll get you killed. You hear me?"

I heard.

Grimes dragged me a couple of blocks from the house to a street corner where the new Zorka fast-food franchise was located. (Zorkas are kind of living waffles that look like dirty running shoes, but they taste great and they're even good for you.) We continued on to the crowded parking lot at the rear of the building.

Grimes looked warily in every direction before pointing to an old, rusted, three-wheeled dumpster near the back door. It was emblazoned with layers of colorful graffiti like "KRONE" and "RETURN2ERIS" in balloon-like letters, and squiggly images of what looked like a coiled snake with dozens of stars coming out of its mouth, a heart-shaped planet torn in half and a black eyeball that seemed vaguely familiar. A small, partially-defaced sign on the receptacle's side said: Flipper Waste Disposal & Transportation Co.

"Get in," Grimes said.

Now I'm not the strongest person in the world (or the second or third strongest, if you want to know the truth), so grasping the edge of the big dumpster, pulling myself up with my scrawny arms and propelling myself inside wasn't going to happen. Not without help.

"I'll need a boost," I said.

Grimes muttered something I didn't understand (thankfully), lifted the lid, grabbed hold of my belt and threw me into the dumpster's dark, smelly guts. I landed on about a dozen garbage bags and some cardboard boxes, and rolled into a pool of runny liquid that smelled like urine and stale pineapple.

Ugh.

I lay on my back, closed my eyes and waited to be transported to what I hoped was a less gross and putrid side of the universe.

Oh, and there was one other detail I should probably mention.

"Move your elbow, Chief," a voice said. "I'm trying to drive this thing."

4

Notable Deaths

"I'm not dead, Leo."

"It's a credible source, Alice Jane," Leo said. "She says your body was found washed up in a place called the 'Inside'—wherever that is—and she goes on to say that most of the universe's shoe, handbag and clothing manufacturers are 'in a state of profound shock and mourning.'"

"It's nice to know somebody cares," I said.

"Another news feed is reporting that: 'The lifeless, bloated and mostly unrecognizable body of interstellar tycoon, business mogul and fashion phenom Alice Jane Zelinski was discovered submerged in the Ick early this afternoon. Authorities have not released a cause of death.'"

"Bloated?" I screeched. "Who says I'm bloated?"

I was pissed. If you want to know the truth, I planned to track down whoever was responsible for killing me off and introduce her or him to a hungry Gutrog. And "Bloated"? Seriously? I also wanted to rip the large and small intestines out of that reporter's body and tie them in a bow around his or her neck.

"Listen to this headline: 'Murder or Suicide? The Shocking Truth Behind the Tragic Death of Alice Jane Zelinski.'"

"Maybe I am dead," I said.

I could hear the sound of Leo's fingers dancing across his keyboard.

"Okay, I found an obituary," Leo said. "It has you down as 'Zelinski, Alice Jane' and 'No Photograph Available' and it's under the heading 'Notable Deaths.'"

Leo read:

Zelinski, Alice Jane. Age 17. Long-time resident of Kansas City, Missouri, and, more recently, Warrensberg, Minnesota, Earth, Milky Way Galaxy. Miss Zelinski was the three-time tug-o-war champion of Jackson County, Missouri, and worked briefly for Royal Protein Enterprises LLC. She is probably best known for using her influence and vast wealth to rescue animals, crustaceans and gastropod mollusks from neglect and abuse. She will also be remembered for her tireless efforts to "reimagine the entire universe in different shades of pink" and her highly popular campaign to "bring doughnuts and gift shops to distant worlds and galaxies." Former Ambassador Philbus Trot, a close friend, said, "Miss Zelinski will be sorely missed. I, for one, plan to carry on her legacy and create the Alice Jane Zelinski Foundation so that her memory—and her generosity to those in need, such as myself— will last for an eternity, or longer." Miss Zelinski is survived by her parents, Donald and Marie Zelinski; half-sister, Nardzilla; cat, Genghis; and 413 Zorazeen godchildren (too numerous to mention by name). No service is planned. Miss Zelinski's cremated remains will be returned to her family on Earth.

"That must be why I can't get into my network," I said as I

looked from one "Access Denied" screen to the next. "I've been deleted. I don't exist anymore."

"I suppose all your assets, accounts, properties and credit cards are frozen, too," Leo said.

"So I really am dead," I said.

"As good as," Leo said.

I should have been royally pissed. I mean, everything I owned and managed was gone. But instead, I felt an overpowering wave of peace pass over me. You see, in the past year I'd gotten caught up in all the bureaucracy and responsibility of running the cosmos, and in maximizing the shareholder value of my bazillion companies. It was exhausting and sucked the life out of me, if you really want to know. Somehow I'd lost my way on my journey to become one with the Great Void.

I was free again.

"This article says that, for now, your 'business interests and extensive holdings will be managed by the courts.' It also says, 'According to legal experts, it may be decades before the affairs of the Zelinski estate are resolved.'"

In other words, I was in a holding pattern between real life and virtual death. (Which is a lot better than the other way around.)

"Hold on, that one guy said my body was 'unrecognizable,' right? So how do they know it was me?"

"DNA or dental records, I suppose," Leo said.

"Nobody else has my teeth, Leo."

Except for Nardzilla, of course. She had my DNA and my teeth. But she wasn't bloated and/or dead, either.

"Do you have enemies, Alice Jane?" Leo asked. "Maybe it was murder like that one article suggested." Then he added, "Of someone else, I mean."

Aside from Jeremy Lynn Mansfield, a couple of monsters I

beat up and a former Senior Ergonomic and Fiscal Engineer, there was no one.

Except....

"Philbus Trot," I said through my one-of-a-kind clenched teeth.

"The guy from the obituary?"

"He's a plumber like Cardamon Webb, but he's screwed up practically all of his jobs. On Earth he caused continental drift and wiped out all the dinosaurs and lost two of our moons. And he almost got me killed for real when we closed the Fiz for the second time. Naturally, he took full credit and somehow became an intergalactic superstar and then an ambassador, if you can believe it."

"Wait, there were two other moons?" Leo said. "You never told me that."

"And last year I kind of negotiated him out of...everything. It's how I got all my money."

That's when the doorbell rang.

The remains, I figured. *My* remains.

I hung up on Leo and walked dazedly downstairs, deep in thought. What was going on? Who was dead? Why did everyone think it was me?

At the bottom of the stairs I nearly tripped over a broken china cabinet. Clearly, Wilkin had done a piss-poor job of cleaning up before he went off to war. The walls and furniture had been destroyed and the place was a shambles.

Just beyond what used to be the front door, a smiling UPS driver stood on the porch holding a cardboard box about the size of a basketball.

"I need a signature, Miss," he said, momentarily distracted by the carbonized shapes swimming in my face and arms, and then

22

handing me a tablet to sign.

"Whatever," I said, wondering if my signature still worked.

"Remodeling?" he asked, looking past the splintered doorway and into the wrecked living room.

"Something like that," I said, taking the package.

I walked back into the house, carefully holding the box. The label said simply: "To: The Family of Alice Jane Zelinski."

I broke the seal and pulled back the flaps.

Inside was a heavy-duty plastic bag full of gritty pink dust like sand. Underneath that I found a one-page form letter and a small manila envelope with the words "Personal Effects" handwritten in block letters on the outside.

I nervously opened the envelope and emptied the contents into my hand: A silver chain and two pink identification tags stamped with a name. My name.

I stared at the tags, then swallowed hard.

I remembered the last time I'd seen them. And the promise I'd made.

My eyes filled with tears.

"Jasper," I whispered to myself.

5

Digger

I moved my elbow. (Both of them, just to be safe.)

"Sorry," I said, hoping I didn't offend whoever or whatever was driving the dumpster.

"You the 'Secret Weapon'?" the driver asked.

"I'm Wilkin Delgado, if that's what you mean," I said, clearing a lettuce leaf and half-eaten Zorka from the general area of my left ear.

Thanks to gravity, an itch in the small of my back, the dry heaves and a constant vibration from the dumpster's engine, I'd pachinkoed down into the stinky depths of that Flipper, and was wedged between a broken peach crate and five garbage bags filled with Zorka waste.

It was not comfortable.

"You like Fanta?" the driver asked. "This planet has all four flavors, you know. Including strawberry."

I shook my head.

"Better get what you can now, Chief. At the FEBA, you'll be lucky to find a stale roll and a bit of possum drool to wash it down with. Just saying."

My appetite was already gone, and the thought of even a sip of possum anything made my esophagus close up fast.

"So you're like the pilot?" I asked.

"Pilot, steward, mechanic, ticket taker, dancing showgirl, you name it," he said. "Call me Digger." He turned his head to look me over. "What do they call *you*, Chief?"

"Wilkin Delgado, like I said," I said.

Once my eyes adjusted to the dim light, I was able to identify a seated, human-like shape about four feet tall with yellowish skin and a large, egg-shaped head topped with a bundle of squirming worm-like "hairs" tied in a ponytail. He had a thin mouth, unblinking violet eyes, sticks for arms and legs, and "hands" and "feet" that resembled animated pretzels.

"Sorry, I probably wasn't listening. Or paying attention. Or maybe I was someplace else. It happens. What was the question?"

"Are you…human?" I asked, skipping over the fact that I hadn't asked a question.

"Human-*oid*, I guess you could say. Got all the same parts— or at least I think I do—just a little more there and a little less here," Digger said, pointing to various regions of his anatomy. "Happy to know you, Chief. The feeling's mutual, I'm sure."

"When do we leave for the Flipside?" I asked.

"What's the rush?" Digger said, swiveling his seat to face me. "Gotta enjoy life while you got it. Care for a Fanta?" He held out a bottle. "It's strawberry."

"No," I said.

I just wanted to get moving.

"Believe me, the war'll still be there when we get back," Digger said. "Always is."

"Where did Grimes go to?" I asked.

"You mean Sarge? Probably stocking up for the ride back," Digger said. "Or looking for that deadly assassin that's been tracking us."

"Assassin?" I said cautiously.

"Yesterday I was a miserable recruit shivering-scared in the FEBA, and set to go into my first—and probably last—battle. But Sarge walks by and says to me, 'You got a choice, Digger. You can die quick, or you can take this Flipper to the dead center of the universe and pick up a special "package."'" Digger looked down at me and smiled. "Like you's some kind of Amazon shipment or something," he said.

He paused.

"That was supposed to be funny," he said.

I tried to laugh, but I was confused and scared and tired and still a little sick.

"Now I ain't the stupidest bulb, so I volunteered to visit historic Warrensberg, Earth, right there at the Octipoint—coordinates 0, 0, 0, like they say—and enjoy the sights and sounds, and get in some practice time flying this rig," he said. "That answer your question?"

It didn't.

"You mentioned something about an…assassin," I said, trying to turn the conversation back to where it started. "Who's he—or she—trying to kill?"

"Our 'Secret Weapon,' more than likely," Digger said. "That'd be you, Chief."

Me?

"Why would anybody want to kill me?"

"Lots of reasons," he said. "With you on our side of the war, right there half of everybody wants you dead."

"I really don't care which side…," I sputtered.

26

"And the whole idea of a Secret Weapon is that it'll win the war for us. So naturally they're opposed to that line of thinking."

Naturally.

"Shouldn't a Secret Weapon be a secret?" I asked.

"You'd think so. But it's in all the papers and on the feeds and channels," he said. "You're practically a celebrity."

Great.

Everybody on the Flipside knew I was coming (even before I did), believed I was some kind of miracle cure to end the war (which I wasn't) and there was a ruthless assassin out there trying to kill me (which was more than a bit unsettling).

I needed a good place to hide. Fast.

"So can this thing actually fly?" I asked.

"Doesn't so much 'fly' as shimmy its way through the cellular structure of the universe. Like going through a slippery dark ventricle and coming out the other end, but all turned around," Digger said.

I didn't have a clue what he was talking about.

"It looks, um, old," I said, just to say something.

"Seasoned, I guess you'd call it," Digger said. "Three or four centuries back it was state-of-the-art. Now it's just 'art.' Lost the 'State-of-the-' part somewhere out in the blackness of space. Fell right off."

That's when Grimes leapt into the dumpster and secured the lid.

"Time to go," he said quickly.

"Right you are, Sarge. We was just awaiting your instructions," Digger said. Then he gave me a quick look. "Newbies get the bottom bunk, you know."

I "swam" through the garbage until I reached some rickety metal shelves sticking out from one of the walls. I claimed the bottom shelf and fastened my seat belt as the engine began to grind and whine. After that, I tensed my muscles and gritted my teeth, preparing for a sudden takeoff. (Or explosion.) Instead, the container rose a couple of feet off the ground, and was shaken and pummeled by an unknown force.

"Go," Grimes told Digger.

So we went. Or at least we tried to.

"Got us a barnacle," Digger said.

"A what?" I asked.

"A foreign object that's attached itself to the ship. Could be trouble," Digger said. "Hang on."

The Flipper shot into the air and spun like a corkscrew. The centrifugal force drove me (and my internal organs) flat against the wall so I almost couldn't breathe.

"It's still with us," Grimes shouted.

As soon as he said that, a sharp blade punctured one of the inch-thick metal walls right next to my head, and began to tear open the Flipper like it was a can of Hormel Chili with Beans.

"Is that the Assassin?" I asked, frozen with fear.

"Lose it, Digger," Grimes said. "Or you're back at the front of the front line."

Digger turned a knob and pressed a button on the control panel while he hyperventilated and muttered, "Evasive maneuvers, evasive maneuvers," to himself. That was followed by an ear-splitting screech and a disturbing "ka-chunk," as a cloud of thick, black smoke covered everything, including the insides of my lungs and boxers.

Then, like a violent hiccup, we popped into what I think was the Flipside, after which the Flipper did a nauseating somersault and braked to a sudden stop.

Screech!

The "barnacle" lost its grip, the sharp pointy object vanished and I think I heard an inappropriate curse.

"We're clear," Digger said, calmly taking a sip of Fanta.

The grinding sound of the engine had stopped, and as we began to descend all I could hear was a faint whistle of air through the punctured wall.

I undid my seat belt and listened as my heart slowed to a normal, steady beat.

"This is more like it," I said, finally able to relax. "Nice and peaceful."

"That's because we lost power," Digger said through the black haze. "We're going down. Follow emergency procedures."

"Which are?!!!" I asked in a boomerang of panic.

"Close your eyes, Chief," Digger said.

I closed my eyes.

Seconds later, the Flipper slammed into some hard surface, skidded about a quarter mile on its side and spilled me, Digger and Grimes into the slippery flora and fauna of some otherworldly jungle.

Once I stopped sliding, I rolled onto my back and spit out something gray and crunchy. Then I covered my ears with my hands. All around me there were blasts, screams, swearing and the smell of burning sulfur and death.

"Welcome to the war, Mr. Secret Weapon," Grimes shouted.

6

A Prayer for Jasper

I bowed my head and said a prayer for Jasper.

Om Ami Dewa Hri.

A couple years ago, Jasper and I were part of a six-mile chain of marshmallowy protein Blops holding the universe together on the Inside. (It's a long story.) While we were hanging around and minding our own business, swarms of mosquito-like dachshund-sized protein-eating creatures called Skeedles tried to pick us off and suck the life out of us. As you can imagine, one of those big bugs wanted to snack on Alice Jane Zelinski's heart-stopping beautilicious flesh. (Can you blame it?) But just before that needle-nosed vampire could suck out my protein like I was some kind of Hi-C juice box, Jasper stretched out his body and took the hit instead of me.

He saved my life. And nearly died himself.

Not long after that, Jasper matured and was able to take his place on the chain without my help. Which is when I hung my identification tags around what I think was his neck and said, "I owe you."

That was the last I saw him.

Until now.

"Jasper," I said tearfully, hugging the bag of pink ashes.

Jasper had died and his "bloated" body was found with my nametags, which is why everybody thought it was me. I wiped away my tears and opened the letter inside the box.

It said:

It is my painful duty to inform you that a report has this day been received from the Office of the All and Everything notifying the death of: Alice Jane Zelinski

Cause of death:
Unknown

Personal effects associated with deceased:
• Two (2) pink identification tags (enclosed)
• One (1) silver ball chain (enclosed)

Expressed wishes of deceased:
Unknown

These effects and the remains will be returned to:
The Family of Alice Jane Zelinski

At deceased's most recent address on record:
Warrensberg, Minnesota, Earth, Milky Way Galaxy

With greatest regret.

Officer in Charge of Records:
Mr. Milkin Thodmore Bowen (signature)

What now?

I read that letter over and over, and every time I did, I got stuck on the words "Expressed wishes" and "Unknown."

Jasper deserved better than being found dead and unrecognizable in the sewer of the universe without a name or a history or even a footnote, and with his remains ending up in a plastic bag in crappy Warrensberg, Minnesota.

I stared at the ashes.

"I owe you, Jasper," I said.

If you know anything about me (which you probably don't), you know that when I make a promise, I keep it. No matter what. But with Jasper gone, what could I do? How could I pay back a debt to the dead?

Then I thought of a way.

I sprinted upstairs, kicked off my Uggs and quickly changed into my Eileen Fisher Long Sleeve Organic Cotton Blouse and Anatomie Susan Skinny Ankle Pants. (I looked amazing, as usual.) After that, I spent a few extra seconds deciding on the perfect shoes. (Take care of your feet and your feet will take care of you. That's my motto.) I narrowed it down to: Gucci Marmont Fringe Suede Ballerina Flats (lightweight and comfortable); Tieks Eco Park Polka-Dot Flats (from the Vegan Collection); Nike Free RN Flyknit Running Shoes (for speed and flexibility); L.L. Bean Bar Harbor All-Weather Boots (cold weather classics); and Hunter Refined Back Strap Wellingtons (high fashion and waterproof).

I picked the Tieks, of course. (Polka-Dots. Duh.) After that I stuffed Jasper into the Birkin, grabbed the Iknatian spear and ripped the electronic tracking bracelet off my ankle. (Sorry, Dennis.)

Then I ran.

As I passed through the open doorway of the house, I looked around in a hundred different directions. That's when I spotted the one-armed soldier jumping into a graffitied dumpster at the back of the Zorka franchise three blocks away.

I needed to get inside that dumpster.

You see, my idea was to take Jasper's remains to a better place, so he wouldn't be stuck in Dorkville for an eternity. (Which is about five minutes, if you know what I mean.) But with no money or passport, and being officially dead, I was stuck. Unless I could hitch a ride into outer space with Wilkin and his soldier friend, and figure out something after that.

Like I said, I ran.

In under thirty-three seconds I was standing in front of that waste container, ready to jump inside.

Easy, right?

Nope.

Just as I was poised to open the lid and fly off to never-never land, a magnificent muscled hunk of a warrior stepped in front of me.

"Do not interfere, wench," he said.

Wench? Wench?

Okay, I have to admit he was kind of cute, even if that "wench" comment pissed me off. He stood six feet tall and was dressed to kill (literally) in black leather armor with silver accents and a coordinated black tunic, black leather boots, and a complete arsenal of sharp and deadly weapons. He also had this dreamy mane of blonde curly hair and piercing turquoise eyes. (Turquoise!) And when he smiled—or grimaced, actually—he had one of those little dimples in the middle of his chin. I'm a sucker for those things.

The dumpster clicked, groaned and began to move.

I was out of time.

"Back off, Dimple Man," I said.

"Be gone if you value your life," he said, as his delicate and well-manicured fingers came to rest on the silver-hilted dagger tucked into his belt.

"Ditto," I said, not wasting valuable time with unnecessary words.

As you probably know, I'm a certified graduate of Master Woo's Peace and Power Martial Arts Academy in the Warrensberg Mall. Which makes me an expert at Shaolin Kung Fu. Plus, I'm well on my way to a happy, healthy and enlightened life, and to becoming one with the Great Void.

In other words, nobody messes with Alice Jane Zelinski.

I spun, jabbed him in the gut with the butt end of the Iknatian spear, followed that up with a butterfly twist kick to his throat, and finished with a bone-crunching combination side punch and reverse punch to that little dimple on his pretty face.

In the blink of his two turquoise eyes, Dimple Man was on the ground unconscious with a dislocated jaw and a bloody nose.

Hey, he started it.

I stepped over his prostrate body, took hold of the dumpster and shook and twisted it like it was a jumbo-sized pickle jar with a stubborn lid. All I wanted was for Wilkin to let me inside. Was that too much to ask? Apparently. Because the container suddenly glowed green, gave a little belch and we rocketed into the sky.

I held on. (Of course.)

That dumpster twisted and spun and must have been going Mach 10 or more, which is when I noticed the polish on one of my nails had chipped off.

"Blerk!" I screamed, and plunged the tip of the Iknatian spear into the side of that big garbage can, puncturing the alien metal.

It was my way of asking the driver to kindly pull over and let me inside.

That didn't happen.

Instead, there was a screech and a "ka-chunk" and an

explosion, and we seemed to slide into some nether area of the universe, with plumes of black smoke trailing behind us. After that, the space dumpster bucked and whiplashed me in a thousand different directions, which is how I lost my grip.

I fell fast and hard, and landed in a lumpy gray swamp next to a village of plastic shacks and a field of spindly submerged weeds. Nearby, dreary animals with sad eyes stood ruminating in the mud while a rainstorm pounded us from above.

It was a place of soggy suffering and despair. And it smelled, too.

I raised myself out of the slime, cleared the mud from all three of my eyes and surveyed the area. There was nothing and nobody. And no doughnuts or gift shops, either.

I took one squishy step forward. Then another.

One thing was crystal clear: I'd picked the wrong pair of shoes.

7

FEBA

I felt like a squashed bug.

My body was flattened and floor burned after skidding across the surface of that war-torn world on the Flipside. Every part of me was battered and bruised. But, as far as I could tell, nothing was broken. Or missing.

I stood unsteadily, took a few gulps of rancid air, and cleared out both ear canals with the tip of my little finger.

Then I looked around.

The Forward Edge of the Battle Area was a patchwork of craters, smoldering ruins, discarded weapons and armor, and burning vegetation. Clouds of smoke and dust swirled in every direction like an army of confused ghosts. And cries, blasts, piercing screams and haunting silences supplied the soundtrack.

I was numb.

I didn't know what to expect when I'd "volunteered" to help Cardamon Webb, but this definitely wasn't it. To start with, I don't like the whole *idea* of war. (The killing and negativity, in particular.) I'd rather reason with people and try to get along, if possible. Clearly, that wasn't going to happen.

"Digger," Grimes said, slowly getting to his feet and studying the battlefield through a pair of ancient binoculars. "Take SW to HQ."

I think 'SW' meant Secret Weapon, which meant me.

"This way, Chief," Digger said, diving onto the ground and crawling snake-like on his belly through the underbrush. "And be real careful. If something happens to you, I'm the one that gets in trouble."

"I'll do what I can," I said, slithering after him.

A mortar shell exploded about ten feet away from us, spitting up dirt and taking down trees. Every one of my 206 bones vibrated from the shock.

"What is this place?" I asked, scurrying faster.

"It's part of a big round manufactured planet called Eris," Digger said. "It's covered with jungles and sand and mud—and water that looks like green snot."

"Manufactured? You mean it's fake?"

"Depends on how you look at it," Digger said. "We can walk on it and fight on it and die on it, which makes it just as real as I am."

I pulled a leaf from one of the plants.

"It's plastic," I said.

"Yes, but *real* plastic," Digger said.

Argh.

We slowly worked our way through the jungle, past leafy red plants and trees that looked like giant hairy caterpillars twisting and undulating in the gloom. I don't know how, but Digger was able to see through the fuzzy murk, and when we reached a small hut, he got to his feet and guided me through the door.

Once my eyes adjusted to the light, I was able to make out a globular man bent over a large, rectangular desk. A handwritten note taped to the front of the desk identified him as "Corporal Trux."

"Here you go," Digger said, pushing me forward.

I looked down at Corporal Trux, who scribbled a few words on a piece of parchment and stared at me through thick, round glasses.

"Name," he said.

"Delgado. With a 'D.' I'm Wilkin Delgado from Minnesota. It's my first time on the Flipside, in case you want to know."

Corporal Trux paged through a thick binder and shook his head.

"No. That's not right," he said.

"Do you want to see my library card?" I asked.

I pulled out the card and noticed it was expired. Great.

"You're not on the New Recruits list," he said. He tilted his head and looked sideways at me. "You seem familiar, though. You been here before? Got a brother or sister?"

I shook my head.

"This here is the Secret Weapon," Digger said proudly, jabbing a bent pretzel "thumb" in my direction.

"Really? Yes, yes, you're right. Big story in today's paper about you coming and ending the war and saving us all. An honor, yes, quite an honor," he said. "My name's Trux, like it says on the sign." He pointed to the paper taped to his desk. "I'm the clerk around here as of two hours ago." He removed his eyeglasses and wiped them clean. "If you don't mind my saying, you're not anything like the description." He replaced his glasses and frowned. "We were expecting someone bigger and stronger and more, well, handsome."

"Sorry," I said, wishing I were a little more of all those things, too.

"In any case, you need to be processed," Corporal Trux said.

He handed me a sheet of paper with the title: "Welcome to the War."

"What am I supposed to do?" I asked.

"Read it and sign it."

It said:

We are thrilled to have you as part of our diverse and talented Team. Like all of our highly-capable soldiers, you will start out as a Private, but with hard work—and a little luck!—you may eventually be promoted to Corporal, Sergeant, Lieutenant or even Captain. Getting started is easy. First, you will be assigned to a unit of expertly-trained Soldiers, and supplied with: A uniform, a weapon (sword or axe) and a backpack. Second, you will unquestioningly follow the orders of your superior officers. No exceptions! And third, you will fight as best you can, with the object of defeating the Enemy. That's it. A word of caution, though: War can be dangerous*. And since Your Safety is Our Number One Priority, we urge you to Be Very Careful. Again, thank you for joining our Team. We know you have what it takes to be the best.

And there was a footnote (of course):

All Recruits must sign this Waiver stating that they Knowingly and Voluntarily Accept and Assume Responsibility for All Risks and Dangers that might occur during the Event known as War. They also agree to Indemnify, Defend and Hold Both Sides of the War Harmless from any and all Claims, Actions, Suits, Procedures, Costs, Expenses, Damages and Liabilities, including but not limited to Maiming, Decapitation and Death.

"I don't like the sound of this," I said, reading the paragraph (and footnote) a second time.

"Sign it," Grimes said, pointing to the blank line at the bottom of the page.

I signed.

"There you have it," Corporal Trux said. "You're assigned to unit Blue Alpha 4997.63. The Happy Hippos."

"Thank you. I think," I said.

"Get to know and trust your unit," Corporal Trux said, opening a white plastic box with the words "Medical Supplies" printed on the lid. "They're the only thing standing between you and death itself." Then he jabbed me with a three-inch needle, which was attached to a large syringe filled with brown goo. "Disease prevention, you know. Explosions and sharp objects aren't the only things that can kill you." Next he gave me an identification card that said "Private Delgado" and (in big letters) "Secret Weapon," with his own signature at the bottom. "Now get your equipment, Private. And go out and win the war."

I massaged my vaccinated arm as I followed Digger to the back of the hut, where there were four large, disorderly piles of cast-off military equipment: Brown jumpsuits, cracked leather armor, rusty swords and axes, and backpacks that smelled of alien blood and sweat.

I slipped into the largest of the jumpsuits, which was about five sizes too big in the middle and a foot too short in both the arms and legs; put on a set of loose brown armor that made me look like a baggy dung beetle; stuffed my things into an ill-fitting backpack; and stared at the array of bent and battered weapons.

"These are mostly scrounged from the battlefield," Digger said. "Could come from almost any galaxy."

I picked a sword made of a strange, lightweight metal that crackled and spit fire as soon as I touched it. After a few practice

40

swings, I singed my shoelaces and nearly cut off Digger's ponytail. Which is when I stopped practicing.

"Got a real sharkskin grip on that one," Digger said.

"And duct tape to hold it together," I added.

"Now let me introduce you to our unit," Digger said. "Most of them's new, on account of we're all headed off to die. So don't get too attached, if you know what I mean."

We walked along a narrow path with prickly orange bushes on both sides. After about a mile, the trail opened up to reveal a makeshift camp with a saggy tent, a ring of rocks surrounding a pile of burning plastic twigs, and three listless soldiers.

"Here are the Happy Hippos," Digger said. "That's Scuzz."

He pointed to a short, thin boy in a dirty brown T-shirt who was on his knees sharpening a sword.

"Hi, I'm Wilkin Delgado," I said, putting out my hand.

Scuzz didn't look up or even shrug.

"Loaf is the one on his back looking at the sky," Digger said. "He does that a lot."

Loaf tilted his head in my direction and blinked a couple of times.

"This the guy come to save us all?" he asked with a sigh.

"He's cute," said a woman with a three-foot sword and flaming red hair.

"That's Sal," Digger said.

"Nice to meet everyone," I said. "I hope we can work together and do great things."

"This is war," Loaf said. "It's not unicorns and rainbows, in case you didn't know."

It's the Island of Misfit Toys, I muttered to myself.

"Around back there's someone been asking to see you," Digger said, beckoning me with his pretzel fingers.

41

A few hundred feet later we stood in front of a squat, heavily-fortified building made out of large granite blocks, and guarded by a dozen bored-looking armed guards. The only entrance was a thick steel door.

Digger showed our identification cards to the largest of the guards, after which she opened the door and led me inside.

"Good luck, Chief," Digger said nervously, happy to stay on the outside.

As I ducked to get through the doorway, I brushed away part of a spider's web made with silky strands as thick as dental floss. Faint light from a single window illuminated a wall of black, two-inch-diameter iron bars.

I took three steps forward.

It was a dark, horrible, stinky, ungodly prison cell.

"Good of you to come, Wilkin," said a voice from within.

8

Fashion Emergency

I hate mud.

It's slimy and dirty and gets into everything. And I mean everything. It also messes up your hair and wrecks your perfectly manicured nails. (Including your favorite frostbite-colored gel polish, I might add.) Plus it destroys quality fabrics like organic cotton, French honiara (92% polyamide and 8% elasthane) and European textiles with natural, paraben-free dyes. (My entire outfit, in other words.)

I took a deep, feral breath.

I was stuck on some sloppy, stinking world, standing knee-deep in the middle of a sea of liquid gunk as torrential rains and gale-force winds blasted every part of my dazzling, breathtaking body. I was not happy. (Obviously.) But I was on a mission to pay a debt to a lost friend, so I clutched my handbag and slogged through the muck and headed toward the nearest shack, which looked like a sketchy clothing store or boutique.

"Tell me, Jasper," I said to the ashes inside the bag inside the Birkin, "where would you like to be forever?"

It was a good question.

Where would *I* want to be? Definitely not on this disgusting planet, that's for sure. (Did I mention I hate mud?) Or boring Warrensberg, Minnesota. (Duh.) Probably Kansas City. That's my happy place. But Jasper needed his own spot. Part of a nebula or a star cluster, maybe. Or the spiritual center of the universe, wherever that might be.

I arrived at the flat-roofed shack, which featured an annoyed-looking mannequin wearing black leather armor in the display window. A sign on the door said: Closed.

I knocked.

No answer.

I knocked again.

Still no answer.

As you probably guessed, I don't like to spend my precious time staring at closed doors or anything else that gets in my way. So after almost seven seconds of patient and respectful waiting—dripping and chilled and dirty and miserable, as you know—I looked down at my mud-stained blouse, distressed skinny jeans and squishy sludgy vegan shoes and decided I didn't have much of a choice: It was a fashion emergency.

I ripped the flimsy plastic door off its hinges and walked into a cozy, ten-foot-by-eight-foot shop with a small counter and register. Nearly every square inch from floor to ceiling was taken up with shelves of polished leather armor and chain mail and weapons and boots and belts and helmets that were all neatly stacked and organized.

It was like a Gap store for killer warriors.

"Hello?" I said. "Anybody here?"

I set down my spear, lowered the Birkin to the floor and peeled off my shoes. A puddle of muddy water pooled around my dirty, pruny feet.

"What do you want?" a voice said.

"A place to wash up and get some clean clothes," I said. "Preferably a quality name brand like Lululemon, Anatomie, Eileen Fisher or Gucci."

"You got money?" she said.

It was definitely a she.

"You have a name?" I asked.

"Shem."

"Look, Shem, I'm Alice Jane Zelinski LLC," I said. "I just got dumped onto this godforsaken stinking mud pit of a planet—no offense—and I could use a serious bath and a change of clothes. Do you have a loofah, a little floral-scented body wash and maybe a jar of Herbivore Botanicals Coconut Milk Bath Soak around here?"

"We don't have a tub," she said. "Or loofahs."

What kind of gross and uncivilized world had I fallen into?

"I have money. Lots of it." Then I paused, remembering what happened earlier that day. "Or I did. Before I died, that is."

A bored, gum-chewing clerk came out from behind one of the shelves, shaking her head in disgust. She looked to be about nine or ten years old and a little more than half my height, with black skin, green eyes, orange lips and frizzy hair. Above her waist she wore full body armor, but below that she had on blue Pikachu pajama bottoms and fuzzy gray animal slippers.

"We're not Goodwill, lady," Shem said with a sigh. "This is the Flipside, you know."

I didn't know.

I handed her my American Express Platinum Card and waited, hoping my money was good on this side of the universe.

"AmEx says you're dead," Shem said matter-of-factly.

"I'm not," I said.

"Might as well be," someone said.

I looked down at Shem's legs. Her left foot looked up at me.

"Your foot is talking," I said to Shem.

Definitely not my day.

"It's my prosthesis," Shem said, hiking up her pajama legs and showing off a skinny right leg wearing a bunny slipper, and a long, fuzzy, otter-like critter holding onto the stump of her missing left leg. "On account of the war."

"Got it," I said.

What do you say when someone's replacement leg is a talking otter? "Got it" was the best I could do.

"So, Alice Jane Zelinski LLC"—Shem looked back and forth between me and my credit card—"what happened to you?"

"I got thrown off a flying dumpster and landed in your swimming pool out there."

"I mean your skin. It's all spinning and swirly," she said, reaching up to touch my cheek. "It's...pretty."

"I got carbonized by sixty septillion joules of electricity," I said. "Give or take."

"Did it hurt?"

"I don't remember much," I said. "I suppose."

Okay, I'd pretty much had enough small talk.

"Look, it's been fun, but I need to get out of here and find a good place to bury my friend."

"Friend?" she said, wasting even more of my time.

"Inside my bag," I said, picking up my mud-encrusted pink porosus crocodile skin handbag. "He's the one that's dead, not me. His name's Jasper."

Shem pointed to two shoeboxes next to the door.

"My mom and dad, too."

"What happened to them?" I asked.

"The war," she said with a shrug.

Shem walked out from behind the counter. She moved gracefully, effortlessly, like a dancer or ninja.

"Look, I just need some clean clothes," I said. "And a mani and pedi, if it's not too much trouble."

"You're gonna need more than that," Shem said, taking my measurements with a well-used yellow and black tape measure. "You'll be dead for real without a full set of body armor." She made quick notes on a small pad of paper. "Leather corset. Chain mail shirt. Bracers. Leather pants and skirt. Boots. Hand-forged sword. Belt. And wool undergarments from the finest Sezarian sheep."

I pulled a pair of rough leather leggings off one of the shelves.

"Got any yoga pants in this?" I asked.

Shem shook her head.

"Anything in pink?" I asked.

"Black," Shem said.

Figures.

That depressing, muddy Flipside world definitely needed some major fashion improvements. And bath products.

"You got anything to wash up with?" I asked as Shem darted across the store assembling my new outfit.

She tossed me a slightly damp hand towel.

"Here," she said.

"Got more issues than personal hygiene, in my opinion," Shem's left leg said.

I gave that annoying critter one of my if-you-keep-this-up-I'll-skin-you-alive looks, which quieted it down. Then I cleaned myself off as well as I could and put on the underwear, which hung like an oversized tablecloth on my flawless, runway model body.

47

After that, Shem helped me get into the squeaky leather warrior princess outfit. She paused to stare at the eyeball tattoo on the back of my neck (I stared right back), then she cinched straps and buckled buckles and tightened laces until the fit was perfect. I flexed my muscles and practiced swinging the unfamiliar sword. Everything was surprisingly light and flexible.

"You look badass, lady," Shem said, stepping back and looking me over.

"I *am* badass," I said. I eased the sword into the scabbard, and picked up my handbag and spear. "I don't have cash."

"There's no charge," Shem said. "Since you're dead."

I liked her attitude.

"One last thing," I said. "I need to find a good place to bury my friend. So just point me toward the nearest sacred or mystical ground and I'll be gone."

"Wait," Shem said, putting black leather leggings over her pajamas, belting on an assortment of weapons, pocketing a phone, and loading up a large bag with a few essentials plus the shoeboxes with the remains of her parents. "I'm coming."

Seriously?

"Sorry, kid," I said. "I travel alone."

"So do I," Shem said. "We're traveling alone together."

9

EOE 2.0

"I am in need of your assistance once again, Wilkin," Cardamon Webb said through the thick, black bars of his prison cell.

"I kind of guessed that," I said.

In the meager light inside that miserable Flipside fortress, the intergalactic plumber appeared thin and pale, with hollow eyes and skin that looked as fragile as a dragonfly's wings. Rusty iron shackles and chains hobbled his arms and legs. His orange jumpsuit sagged, his feet were bare and his Cleveland Indians baseball cap had a large bite taken out of the brim. Still, his two different-colored eyes were bright and alive.

"I would have come to Warrensberg myself, but I have been detained here for an undetermined period of time." He sighed. "I trust Grimes treated you well?"

"He didn't dismember me, if that's what you mean," I said.

"Good, good."

"Where's Loretta?" I asked, examining the shadowy corners of the plumber's cage.

Loretta is the talking puffin who saved my life a couple of times. Her vocabulary is usually limited to a few brief sentences—"Uh-oh" and "Look out!" for example—which aren't very helpful. She also has a special certificate that says she's a Certified Tracking Puffin (CTP), meaning she can find people and things better than normal puffins, I suppose.

"Away," Cardamon Webb said.

"So what's this about me being a 'Secret Weapon'?" I asked.

"I needed a way to get you to Eris quickly," he said. "This is a matter of some urgency, as you probably guessed."

"So you made that up?" I said. "Everybody thinks I'm here to end the war. And I'm on all the TV channels and newspapers."

"It could not be helped, I am afraid," he said.

"So what's going on? Is there a plumbing disaster that needs fixing?" I asked.

"In a manner of speaking," he said. "You see, some time ago we discovered a trail of missing parts and pieces in the cosmic infrastructure—the piping and sluiceways and canals that distribute waste to the Inside. We also received reports of several billion backed up toilets and clogged drains stretching from one end of the universe to the other."

It sounded disgusting.

"And?" I said.

"Since then we have been working diligently to track down the cause, which led us here to the Flipside and Eris."

"What did you find?"

"Two rather serious problems, I am afraid," Cardamon Webb said.

"More backed up toilets?"

"Worse than that, Wilkin," he said. "It appears that we are all being sucked into the blackest black hole imaginable."

I didn't like the sound of that.

"Also," the plumber continued, "the Doris Supercluster, which is about twenty million light years in diameter and contains about 3,000 galaxies, is gone. Nobody knows where."

Didn't he ever deliver any good news?

"Are we talking about the End of Everything again?" I asked. He nodded.

I nearly threw up.

You see, every time Cardamon Webb asked for my help, we were always on the verge of some major life-threatening, universe-ending disaster. (EOE.) Couldn't he just drop by once or twice to ask for my assistance with a lost puppy or ingrown toenail?

"So what are we doing here?"

"Our data show that Eris has been traveling in a linear rather than elliptical path, and leapfrogging from one galaxy cluster to another for at least 5,000 years," Cardamon Webb said. "Just before slipping into the Flipside, Eris passed by the area where the Doris Supercluster used to be. As near as we can tell, that was about the same time a powerful black hole began to consume the universe."

"You think somebody here on Eris might have seen something?"

"Probably," Cardamon Webb said.

"Or done something?"

"Possibly."

"Like create a mega black hole or steal a supercluster?" I asked.

"There are an infinite number of possibilities, Wilkin."

"This is kind of a big problem for the two of us to handle," I said. "Three if you count Loretta."

"And what of Miss Zelinski?" he asked.

"Back in Warrensberg with her fancy purses and shoes."

"That is unfortunate," he said.

Or not.

I mean, there wasn't much for Alice Jane to do except get in the way. The universe was being sucked into the blackest black hole in history, and there was a rogue supercluster zipping around somewhere in the universe. Alice Jane's crazy Kung Fu moves and big pink purse wouldn't be much help with any of that. And her bad attitude would slow us down and get on my nerves. In my opinion, we were better off without her.

"Maybe the Doris Supercluster was sucked into the black hole," I said.

"A good guess, Wilkin," Cardamon Webb said. "But no."

"What about the war?" I asked. "What are we supposed to do about that?"

"It is not our problem," Cardamon Webb said.

Finally a bit of good news.

I really hated to ask the next question, but I needed to know what Cardamon Webb's words "matter of some urgency" meant, especially since I had no idea what I was supposed to do or where I was supposed to go.

"How much time do we have?" I asked.

"According to our best models, the universe is converging—swirling into that black hole like water down a bathtub drain, if you will—at an ever-increasing rate of speed."

"How much time?" I repeated.

"About six days, I should think," Cardamon Webb said. "Which is why it is one of our top ten priorities right now."

Argh.

"So where do we even start?" I asked. "I mean, I'm just a sixteen-year-old kid with an expired library card."

"You have the Key?"

A couple of years back Cardamon Webb gave me the Key to the City of the Dead for safekeeping. He told me it's the only true skeleton key in existence. It will open any lock—once.

"You want me to get you out of prison so you can fix everything?" I said hopefully, fingering the leather cord around my neck.

"Heavens, no," he said. "I am much safer in this cell than anywhere else."

"So what do you want me to do?" I asked.

"I have great faith in your abilities, Wilkin," Cardamon Webb said.

"Which means?"

"You will figure something out," he said.

10

Community Service

"Is there a restaurant or Starbucks nearby?" I asked Shem.

As we hiked along a dark and muddy path trying to find a special burying ground for Jasper, I realized I hadn't eaten anything since Warrensberg. (I'd been kind of busy, as you know.) Looking around, it was pretty obvious there were no Olive Gardens or Red Lobsters within spitting distance. And no Kansas City barbecue joints, either.

Shem bent down and broke off a couple of fuzzy gray weeds growing out of the ground, handed me one and began chewing the other.

"We call them sprouts," she said. "There's always some around, so we never have to worry about food."

I took a bite.

It was like chewing on a squirrel's tail, but the taste was sweet and satisfying in an it's-better-than-starving-to-death kind of way. It definitely could have used a little Grinders Death Nectar hot sauce. (Which I forgot to bring along. Again.)

Not having to worry about food was a real plus. On the minus side, the wool of the Sezarian sheep isn't as soft and cloud-like as it's made out to be. In fact, it's scratchy and prickly and smells like a barnyard, and it gives you an itchy rash all over your shapely, perfectly-toned derrière.

Just saying.

"So where are we going?" I asked.

"The Krone," Shem said.

"Krone? What's that?" I asked.

"The last of the Ancients," she said. "She knows things."

"What kinds of things?" I asked.

"Old."

Not helpful.

"Okay, so where does this 'Krone' person live?"

"We call it Ga-da-nor or Ga," she said. "It means, 'The place that isn't.'"

Seriously?

"Don't go there. Too dangerous," her left leg gargled through the mud.

I looked at the leg and then at the girl.

"The reviews I'm hearing aren't all that positive," I said.

"You have to cross the Field of Blood is why," she said.

"That doesn't sound safe," I said.

"You got that right," her left leg said.

"It's what happened to my parents," Shem said quietly. "And me."

There had to be a better way to find a good resting place for Jasper—one that didn't involve all of us (especially me) dying.

"Where is this bloody battlefield?" I asked.

"Starts about...," Shem said.

An explosion sent boulders and mud flying in our direction. We dove to the ground and rolled underneath the trunk of a huge fallen tree.

"Here," she finished.

"And this Ga place that doesn't exist?" I asked, guessing the answer to that one as well.

"Somewhere on the other side of the Field of Blood," Shem said. Of course.

We huddled together on the edge of the battlefield for at least an hour. Bombs dropped and shells burst. Trees became splinters. Rocks became gravel. And clouds of chalky smoke wrapped us in a thick and anxious shroud.

As we waited, I heard someone scream for help in the distance. That was followed by a chorus of at least a dozen heart-rending cries and shrieks.

There was a lot of pain out there.

"Who's fighting?" I asked.

"There's new soldiers every day," Shem said. "Most never come back."

"What about weapons? I didn't see any guns in that shop of yours," I said.

"Just axes and swords," Shem said. "That's all we use."

"But there's bombs and explosives."

"It's the war, Alice Jane," Shem said. "That's the way it's always been."

Deep within the Field of Blood there was another cry for help. And then another.

Look, it wasn't my planet or my war, but I didn't like the idea (or reality) of anyone bleeding or legless. Or ending up as dust in a shoebox, either. I thought about Jasper's remains stuffed in my handbag, waiting to find some kind of eternal resting place. And I thought about his courage and sacrifice. I would have died without him.

That was all it took.

I rolled out from under the tree trunk, sloughed off a layer of mud, gritted my teeth, hefted the Iknatian spear and charged through the muck toward the sounds of battle and cries of pain and fear, one squishy slurpy step at a time.

"What are you doing?" I heard Shem call out.

"Community service," I growled.

If you want to know the truth, I hated everything about my restraining orders and house arrest, and especially having to smile and be nice to the Warrensberg City Council and Dennis. (I wanted to tear their heads off, actually.) But my social worker Carol kept after me, saying, "Helping is healing," which sounded like one of Master Woo's mantras. So as part of my 10,000 hours, I picked up litter, gave out food at the food shelf, cleaned up doo-doo at the animal shelter and even shoveled Mrs. Itasco's sidewalk. And you know what? Carol was right. I felt better. Which pissed me off.

I sped across the field while the earth vomited mud and rained plastic chunks and pellets. I was taking a big risk, but, for good or bad, I'd made a decision. I had to do something. I couldn't sit around on my duff waiting for an entire army of women and men to die.

Twelve minutes later, I spotted a man crying out in pain and holding his chest. I grabbed him by the collar without even stopping.

"Where's a hospital?" I shouted, seizing a second soldier whose head was covered in blood.

"About a mile ahead," Shem yelled back.

"If we live that long," Shem's left leg said.

I scooped up a third leather-clad soldier. This one clutched her arm, part of which was missing. I stopped to make a tourniquet out of her shredded tunic and kept going.

In that last long mile, blasts of death fell from the sky and everything around me erupted in crimson fire. I picked up two more injured soldiers as I stormed across the Field of Blood, dodging explosions and sprinting toward what I hoped was safety and help.

"I'm going to die, aren't I?" the young man in my arms said.

"You got a bad attitude, kid," I said.

I increased my pace, weaving around smoking craters and through the driving rain and deadly bursts that rocked the ground. That's when I noticed a couple hundred terrified soldiers forming a ragged, snaking line behind me.

"Hospital's up ahead on your left, Alice Jane," Shem said.

"Got it," I said, spying a tattered white flag with a big red cross on a distant flagpole.

I kept focused on the flag until I finally charged through a thicket of dense plastic foliage and burst into a makeshift hospital that was somehow insulated from the noise and destruction of the war.

"Medic!" I screamed, dropping to my knees and gently setting the five bloody soldiers onto the ground.

Doctors and nurses swarmed around me and carried the wounded away.

After that, the hundreds of exhausted, wet and shabby warriors who'd followed me crowded into the hospital and collapsed in a heap.

I stood, looked down and watched thick rivulets of blood slide off my leather bodice and drop into the puddles at my feet, turning the water an unholy shade of pink.

"You're one crazy lady, Alice Jane," Shem said, shaking her head.

I glanced up at the flagpole. At the top sat a small black bird with a white breast and orange beak and feet. She shook her head, too.

"Loretta?" I said.

11

Jot

I stepped out of the darkness and stench of that Flipside prison and came face-to-face with floodlights, cameras, applause and (unfortunately) fame.

"Tell us, Mr. Delgado," said a small woman in a rhubarb-colored blazer, white blouse, short black skirt and pageboy haircut, as she thrust a microphone into my face, "what does it *feel* like to be famous?"

"Um…huh?" I answered, my eyes blinking.

"Reggie, I need a close-up," the woman said to a nearby cameraman as she adjusted her hair. He gave her a "thumbs up." She looked at the camera, smiled and said, "This is Jotheran Olivia Tropacana with an *exclusive* interview. Right now I am *live* at the FEBA talking to our own Secret Weapon, a.k.a., Wilkin Delgado of the Milky Way galaxy." She turned to me. "Welcome to Eris, Mr. Delgado."

"Thanks…um…Ms. Tropacana," I said, trying to be polite as I shielded my eyes from the glare.

"Call me Jot. It's so much easier," she said in an overly-familiar manner. "Let's cut to the chase. Tell me, Wilkin, what are your plans to end the war?"

Plans?

"I don't…I'm really not all that concerned with the war," I said.

As you know, I had other things on my mind. Like having just six days to work out how to stop the universe from being sucked into a black hole. And there was also that missing supercluster. But, according to Cardamon Webb, I didn't have to worry about the war.

"He's 'Not concerned,' he says." Jot laughed. "Now that's confidence, wouldn't you say?" she said to the crowd. They cheered. "It's just business-as-usual for the Secret Weapon." More cheers.

"I'm serious," I said nervously.

"Can't give away all your secrets, is that it?" Jot said with a smile.

I noticed Grimes, Digger, Scuzz, Loaf and Sal among the crowd.

"Is that your unit?" Jot said.

"The Happy Hippos," I said.

"Reggie, you got that? Over here. Medium shot." Jot grabbed me by the arm and dragged me to the out-of-the-way spot where my unit was standing side-by-side. "Sergeant Grimes, is it?" she said, reading the nametag on Grimes' uniform. "What do you think of our new arrival?"

"Asks a lot of questions. Doesn't know a thing about fighting," Grimes said. "But he hasn't done any harm, either. Not yet."

"Private Digger?" Jot said, moving down the line.

"It's like I was saying, Miss," Digger said. "There's two kinds of people in this world, and he's one of them." He looked at me.

60

"Right, Chief?"

I nodded.

"And you…Private Loaf?" Jot asked.

"He's full of himself," Loaf said.

"Private Salanatwicz?" Jot said to Sal, passing up Scuzz, who was quietly sharpening his sword.

"He's dreamy," Sal said, grabbing my arm and giving me a hug.

"Close-up here, Reggie. On me," Jot said, turning to speak directly to the camera. "And there you have it. Our first look at Private Wilkin Delgado of the Milky Way galaxy, the 'Secret Weapon' who's come to deliver us from our 2,500-year-old war. Wish him well, everyone."

Cheers.

"And…cut," Jot said.

The crowd rushed me and tore at my clothes and thrust paper and pens into my face, demanding autographs and asking for money. Somebody even kicked me. (I think it was Loaf.)

After about five minutes, Jot pulled me aside.

"That was amazing, Wilkin, amazing," she said. "Of course, there's more we can do. And makeup…we'll have to worry about that. And some of your backstory. Were you tormented as a youngster? Lost a mother or father?"

"No," I said. "Well, my dad did disappear to Taiwan or California when I was ten."

"That's what I'm talking about," Jot said, making some quick notes.

I looked over at Grimes, Digger, Scuzz, Loaf and Sal.

"I need to get with my unit, Miss … Jot … ma'am," I said.

"No worries," she said. "Reggie and I are officially embedded with the Happy Hippos, so we're one big family now. It'll allow us to get the full story of 'How I Ended the War As Told to Jotheran Olivia Tropacana.' I'm thinking bestseller, Wilkin."

"Hooray," I said weakly.

"Get over here, Delgado," Grimes snapped. "We have a war to fight, if it's not too much trouble."

"Are we going into battle?" I asked.

"Our assault mission has been cancelled," Grimes said, disappointed. "The higher-ups don't want any bad PR of you getting killed and all—especially live on TV—so we're stationed here for the foreseeable future."

That was good news.

"Then if it's not too much trouble," I said, "I need to find out a few things."

"Listen, Private," Grimes said, grabbing me by the collar. "You're now living in my world. That means I make the rules. Got that?"

"I do, but...," I said, searching the sky for a sign of our impending doom.

"No 'buts,'" Grimes said.

"I'm just trying to find out what's going on," I said. "Is there a map or history book or anything?"

"Talk to Sal," Grimes said, pushing me away and shaking his head.

I tracked down Private Salanatwicz, who was schmoozing with Reggie the cameraman.

"Do you have a minute, Sal?" I asked.

"I got all day for *you*, Sugar," she said. "What do you need?"

"A map," I said. "I'd like to get a better idea of where we are and what's happening with the war. Sergeant Grimes said you might know."

Sal went to her backpack and pulled out an old, rolled-up

piece of paper, then dropped to the ground and called me over.

"I'm the navigator for the Hippos," she said, unraveling and flattening the scroll. "The rest of these jokers couldn't find the toilet without me."

I sat down next to Sal and studied the map.

"So where are we?" I asked.

"Here," Sal said, using a stubby index finger with a gnawed, unpainted nail to point to a small dot in the center. "And this red line"—she traced a straight path from one side of the map to the other—"is the FEBA."

"Okay. So above the red line is…?"

"The enemy scum," she said.

"And we're below the red line?"

"That's right," she said. "What else you want to know?"

"What about advances and retreats, wins and losses?" I said. "That would change the whole battle landscape, wouldn't it?"

"The line never moves," she said.

I gave her my normal confused look.

"What's this war about, Sal?" I asked.

She shrugged her shoulders.

"It's war," she said.

That's exactly what Grimes had told me.

I rubbed my temples and tried to think. People were fighting and dying, but nobody knew why. And the battle lines never moved. Ever. Even after 2,500 years.

My brain hurt.

"What does the enemy look like?" I asked.

Sal shook her head.

"Never seen one of them directly. But they're out there. You can hear them. Smell them. Mean little crappers, too. Killed my baby brother."

63

None of it made any sense.

"You ever look up at the stars, Sal?"

"I don't care about stars," she said. "I'm just trying to hold onto life as long as I can."

"I know what you mean," I said.

"So what's the big plan?" she asked.

I told her the truth.

"The war will be over in six days," I said. And then added to myself, "Along with everything else."

12

The Only Caring Person

Loretta soared down from the flagpole, circled around my head and landed on a faded plastic sign that said: Medical Personnel Only.

"Is Webb here, too?" I asked.

She nodded.

"To help end the war?"

She shook her head.

Of course not. My guess? Our favorite intergalactic plumber was more worried about how to unclog a cosmic toilet or remove a giant celestial bathtub stain. He didn't care about little things like war and death and dying.

"We're looking for a place that doesn't exist," I said to the bird. "Can you help?"

Loretta rolled her eyes. Then she nodded.

That's when I noticed Shem and several hundred wet and stinky soldiers gathering around me. (And invading my beautilicious space, I might add.)

"What do you want?" I said.

"To thank you," Shem said.

"For what?"

"Saving their lives," Shem said like I was stupid.

"Whatever," I said.

As I've said before, I don't do well with all that "Thank you" and "You're welcome" garbage. It's a lot of wasted breath, if you ask me.

"You saved us, Miss," someone said.

"We were as good as dead," someone else said.

"You're the first one that's ever cared," a third someone said.

Seriously?

Let me just say that things on Mud World were in really bad shape if I was the only caring person they'd ever met. You see, I care more about gastropod mollusks than human beings. People are what's wrong with the world. That's been my philosophy since forever, and I've never seen it proved otherwise.

"Tell me, who's in charge of this stinking war?" I asked.

"Captain Tagg," one of them said.

"Where is he?" I asked.

They pointed toward a large, expensive-looking house on top of a nearby hill.

I hiked up the road to the three-story red brick building and pounded on the door. A few seconds later, a large, out-of-shape man in a black uniform appeared. One side of his dress coat was covered with medals, the other identified him as Capt. Tagg.

"Yes?" he said, looking at my mud-caked boots and bloodstained armor, and probably smelling my scratchy wool undies.

"I got a problem with this war of yours," I said. "Three problems, actually."

You see, in my approximately twenty-four hours as a visitor

on that godforsaken planet, I'd already noticed some freaky weird stuff about the battlefield and the war. So I (foolishly) ignored my own good advice and (stupidly) decided to get involved.

"Go away," Captain Tagg said.

"Problem one," I said, "every week you're sending hundreds—maybe thousands—of soldiers into the battlefield to die." Tagg's face was blank and unmoving. "Problem two, your army's only weapons are swords and axes, but they're being killed by shelling and explosives." Tagg blinked once and sighed. "And problem three, it's been going on for years. And nobody knows why. And nobody seems to care. Especially you."

Nothing.

"Finished?" he said finally.

"Almost," I said. "I'm stopping this war of yours right now. No more attacks. We'll set up a line of defense on this side of the battlefield and just sit tight and see what happens."

"You have no authority," Captain Tagg said dismissively.

I turned to the growing mass of soldiers that had formed behind me.

"Nobody goes back onto the battlefield, do you hear me?" I shouted.

The soldiers dropped their weapons and cheered.

"I will see that you are court-martialed and beheaded, Miss," Captain Tagg said.

"I'm not in your blerking army," I said.

He paused and licked his lips.

"Then my associate will deal with you," he said, raising his right hand and snapping his fingers three times. He added, "Please excuse me. I am not fond of violence."

Captain Tagg closed the door in my face.

Just as I was about to rip the door off its hinges and eviscerate the Captain with my pinky fingernail, I heard a murmur of voices and a rustle of leather as the crowd parted. Next, a tall hunk of a warrior in black armor strode toward me across the open path. As he got close, his expression quickly changed from annoyance to recognition to hatred. Then he pulled a pair of gleaming swords from two scabbards belted onto his back and pointed them in my direction.

Me? I smiled when I saw the dimple on his chin and the discoloration of his beautiful broken face.

"You," he snarled through a wired-shut jaw.

"Alice Jane Zelinski LLC," I said.

He sliced the air with the swords as he walked nearer and nearer, approaching at an angle, stalking me like a cat. (Which reminded me of how much I missed Genghis.)

I didn't really want to fight, but I didn't have a choice. (As usual.) So I bowed; said a prayer; tossed my sword, sheath and Birkin (with Jasper) to Shem; and dropped into a forward stance. I cradled the Iknatian spear in my two hands.

"Extend my greetings to Death, wench," he sneered.

Again with the 'wench'?

Then he attacked.

I kept low and used the shaft of the spear to deflect his first and second sword thrusts, after which I countered with an uppercut to his right wrist with the spear tip—sending one sword flying—followed by a chop to his right knee with the butt end of the spear, which knocked him to the ground.

Point Zelinski.

Immediately, he did a backwards flip and limped around me, looking for a weakness. Then he sprang forward, faked a thrust with his remaining sword and drove the toe of his boot into my right side.

That fractured at least two of my ribs.

Ugh.

I took a couple of painful breaths and adjusted my undies.

According to Master Woo, deception is a key teaching of Shaolin Kung Fu. Zigging when your opponent expects you to zag, in other words. It gives you an edge. And so does having an extra eye on the back of your neck. (Thank you, Leo.)

I turned away from Dimple Man, lowered myself to the ground, set my spear in front of me and assumed a position of meditation and prayer. Back straight. Eyes closed. (Mostly.) Mind clear. Then I watched as the killer advanced confidently behind me. He smiled as he raised that three-foot-long sword into the air with both hands, and roared as he brought it straight down at my head like he was slicing a watermelon in half.

He missed.

You see, as soon as that sword began to drop, I spun away from its downward path and brought Dimple Man to the ground with a roundhouse kick to his legs. And I finished him off with a jumping downward elbow strike to the back of his head.

Crack!

He lay facedown in the mud, unconscious, blowing bloody bubbles through a broken nose.

Game over.

Then I turned and headed toward the mountain, with Loretta up ahead in the sky and Shem following close behind.

"He was going to kill you, wasn't he?" Shem said, coming up beside me.

"I suppose," I said.

"Why?"

"Why does anyone kill?"

Good question.

We spent two days working our way up the side of the mountain, following paths that vanished and reappeared. We walked through mud pits, past dangerous cliffs and over patches of slippery rock, and always there was rain and mist and the shadow of a puffin slicing through the darkness above.

"Are we lost?" Shem asked, shivering in the cold and wet.

"No. Loretta is like a bird GPS," I said.

"My mom and dad…we tried to come here once," she said. "Last year when the world was falling apart and everything seemed to be…," Shem said.

"Crumpling."

"You know that?"

"All the worlds and galaxies and matter were coming together," I said. "The life force of the universe had gone away."

"But it came back," Shem said.

"Yeah. That's when I got carbonized," I said, staring at the fractal images swimming inside my hands and arms.

"But everything's normal now, right?" Shem said.

I searched the inscrutable sky.

"I'm not sure," I said.

Cardamon Webb was in the neighborhood. That was never a good thing.

We came through a gap on one side of the mountain, and suddenly the sky cleared and the rain stopped. Up ahead I saw Loretta perched on a rock, talking to a thin, bent, withered woman with black hair streaked with gray. She was covered in layers of diaphanous pink robes and steadied herself with a simple cane. As we approached, she bowed and offered us a smile, the gentle touch of her hand and a glimpse into eyes that went on forever like an eternal light.

"Finally," she said in a crusty, unused voice.

13

The Healer

Groan.

I didn't want my face on magazines or billboards or TVs, but I didn't have a choice. I was the not-so-secret "Secret Weapon," and I was famous, which isn't as fun and exciting as you think. For one thing, people recognize you and want to tell you their life stories. (Or kick you.) For a second thing, everybody wants something from you, especially money. (Which I don't have.) And for a third thing, you can't just slip away unnoticed to stop a black hole from eating the universe alive. (A major problem.)

That morning I woke from a fitful, dreamless sleep after spending the night on the hard ground. My neck hurt, my back was sore and I stumbled around looking for coffee and breakfast. Which is when I saw Jot coming up the path. ("Uh-oh," as Loretta would say.) She elbowed Scuzz and Sal aside, stepped on Loaf, ignored Digger and went right up to Grimes.

"Sergeant," she said, "the General would like a series of patriotic stills of the Secret Weapon for promotional purposes."

Grimes was not happy. He didn't like all the distractions. He

71

just wanted to kill people. And from his look and expression, I was the next one on his list.

"We're trying to win a war, Miss," Grimes snapped.

"And every little bit helps. Thank you for your support, Sergeant," Jot said. She turned to me. "Wilkin, we're looking for something dramatic and inspirational out of you. Something to captivate the crowds."

Reggie squinted at me, then rubbed his forehead in despair.

"Not a lot to work with," he said.

I had to agree.

"Makeup!" Jot screamed. "Ozzie, I need you here right this minute."

A young, red headed man in khakis, brown loafers, a black bow tie and a light blue cashmere sweater raced into camp carrying a three-foot-tall stepladder and a box of lotions, brushes, creams and powders. "Yes, Miss Jot," he said. He planted the stepladder at my feet, climbed up and studied my face. Then he glanced at Jot and shook his head as if to say, "It's hopeless."

What did they expect?

"Attention, people. We have a minor emergency," Jot said, addressing everyone within earshot. "We're taking promo shots in two hours." She paused and waited for some kind of reaction. Then she shouted, "Wardrobe! Lighting! Now!"

The rest was a blur.

About two hours later, we'd relocated to a nearby clearing with a background of mountains, bright sunlight and an unstable flagpole. My face was caked with makeup and I was dressed in a new suit of brown leather armor that almost fit. Plus they gave me a shiny four-foot-long sword that weighed about a hundred pounds, and which I could barely lift off the ground.

Jot clapped her hands together to get everyone's attention.

"Okay, people," she said, "here's my vision. Our Secret Weapon is leading us to victory. Sword held high. Flag in the background. Grim determination on his face. Everybody got that?"

Nods all around.

"A low angled shot will make him look stronger—add drama," Reggie said.

"Do it," she said to Reggie. And to me, "On the ladder, Wilkin."

I dragged the supersized sword over to the stepladder. Along the way, the sharp metal tip made a serpentine mark across the ground.

"We haven't got all day," Jot said impatiently.

"It's heavy," I said.

"Ozzie," Jot said.

Ozzie raced over and helped me climb to the top of the stepladder. Then he steadied my arms as I awkwardly lifted the sword into the air.

"You're on your own now," Ozzie said as he let go and stepped back.

My whole body wobbled while I struggled to keep the sword raised over my head.

"Fearless, Wilkin," Jot barked. "Look fearless."

Over the next twenty-five seconds, I experimented with about a dozen different "fearless" looks, which varied from "pained" to "constipated." I puffed out my cheeks. I gritted my teeth. Sweat streamed down my neck.

I felt dizzy.

That's when this swarm of about a thousand people wearing white robes and chanting strange words converged all around us. As soon as I saw that, I lost my concentration, my center of gravity shifted and I fell. Hard.

I ended up sprawled on my back staring at the sky.

"You get that, Reggie?" Jot said.

"Maybe," he said. "Looked more like he was going to wet himself than lead an army into war, though."

I got to my feet and tried to shake off what was probably a mild concussion.

"It's those Healers, Miss Jot," Ozzie said. "Some kind of religiousy thing, I think."

"Everybody get back," Jot shouted to her crew. "Not you, Wilkin," she said to me. "Here's the story. You journeyed all the way from a distant galaxy to save us all. You're the hope. You're the one they've been waiting for. And the entire Holy Order of the Who-Knows-What comes out to greet you and present their... what is it, Reggie?"

"Looks like a book," Reggie said.

"Doesn't matter," Jot said. "Bow and thank the priest or sage, and say how great it is. Got that?"

"I suppose," I said.

A small boy in a white choirboy robe with face and hands painted a ghostly white pressed through the multitude, carrying a big leather-bound book in his outstretched arms. He moved slowly, like he was observing some kind of ritual. Then the entire Holy Order began a deep and mysterious chant.

"'The Sixteen Sacred Words of Eris,'" the boy announced. "For The Healer."

I held out my hands and accepted the gift. It was almost as heavy as the sword, and about as big as a family size box of Kellogg's Frosted Flakes cereal, but thicker and old-smelling.

"We entrust our sacred text to you," the boy said over the chanting, "who has come to heal our faithless, troubled world."

I bowed and mumbled eight or nine nonsensical words. (Hey,

I was nervous.)

"Zoom in," Jot said.

"What am I supposed to do?" I asked the boy.

"Read," he said.

"You getting this, Reggie?" Jot said.

Reggie gave her a "thumbs up."

As I opened the cover of the book, the leather binding creaked and moaned like it hadn't been touched since before the beginning of time. I skipped over the many pages of Introductions, Forwards and Tables of Contents, until I reached the Title on page eighty-three, which I said out loud: "'The Sixteen Sacred Words of Eris.'" Then I turned the page and read:

I am come.
I am an open heart.
I am the light of a thousand suns.

That was it. Sixteen words, like they said. (I counted.) Of course, there was the Appendix, Afterward, Index, Suggested Reading List and 143 pages of Critical Analysis, too. But it was a bit of a letdown, if you want to know the truth.

"It's kind of short," I said. "What does it mean?"

There was a collective gasp from the thousand white-robed, chanting believers.

"He is not the one," several voices said.

"He is an infidel," a loud voice said.

"He must die!" a louder voice shouted.

What?

"Okay, okay," I said, trying to get everyone to calm down. "I meant to say that I know what it means. It's totally clear. No need to freak on me here."

Life was getting more and more complicated. And dangerous.

"You are The Healer?" the boy asked.

"I guess," I said. "I mean, yes. I heal things. That's what I do."

Everything was happening so fast. I needed time to think.

That didn't happen.

"There is among us a great and wise visitor who desires to give blessing and counsel to The Healer," the boy told me. "He, too, comes from the stars."

Jot got up close to my ear.

"Not to scare you or anything, Wilkin," she whispered, "but supposedly this 'visitor' has been trying to chase you down for a while. They say he exploded half of a galaxy just getting here."

My eyes opened wide.

"Is it the Assassin?" I asked nervously.

"Says he knows you," she said.

"But I don't know anybody," I said.

Except I did.

A man in a flowing white silk robe draped over a two-piece gray pinstriped suit, red scarf and luminous yellow necktie stepped out of the mass of chanting zealots and smiled.

"Mr. Delgado," he said. "Just the person I wanted to see."

I recognized that voice. And that face. And those teeth.

Unfortunately.

"Philbus Trot?" I said.

14

The Place That Isn't

"What is this place?" I asked.

"It isn't," the old woman said.

She was already giving me a headache.

We stood on the side of a majestic snow-topped mountain under an open sky, bathed in the light of about a zillion distant suns and with a view of a calming blue-green lake and fields of colorful wildflowers. It was heaven, if you want to know the truth. Definitely not the grimy goopy miserable world I'd been living in for the past three days.

"You're the Krone lady?" I asked the woman.

"I am," she said. "And you are The One Who Comes to The Place That Isn't. It was foretold."

Excuse me?

"Look," I said, "I'm Alice Jane Zelinski LLC, and I came here to find a good resting place for my friend Jasper. That's it."

I held up my pink handbag.

"Me, too," Shem said, opening up her bag and removing the shoeboxes. "My mom and dad."

"This is not the place you seek," the Krone said.

Loretta looked puzzled. (Join the club.)

"It looks perfect to me," I said, filling my lungs with refreshing mountain air. "Jasper will love the sunlight and clean water and mountain view."

You see, I figured I was "that close" to saying "Happy trails" to Jasper, as soon as I could track down a multi-position reclining beach lounge chair for his ashes.

"This is the starting point," she said. "Your journey will begin here."

Okay, I was getting pissed off again. As you know, a few days ago I'd escaped from Dorkville on a supersonic dumpster. Then I got dropped into a mud pit and wrecked my best pair of vegan shoes. After that I was almost blown up on a bloody battlefield a couple of times. Next I was attacked by a killer warrior with a cute little dimple on his chin. And finally I climbed all the way to the top of this stinking 14,000-foot mountain. And for what? So I could start my journey? I don't think so.

"Look, lady," I said, "I'm going to take a bath in that big lake of yours, find a doughnut shop and a drink with a little umbrella, and kick back and enjoy life for the next few days. After that I'll scout out a place for Jasper and Shem's parents, and then head for home so I can finally enjoy some peace and quiet, since I'm dead and all."

"That sounds wonderful," she said.

"I think this is where she says, 'But…,'" Shem's left leg said.

"Yep," Loretta agreed.

"I am sorry, but the lake is not a lake. The sky is not a sky," the Krone said. "This—all of this—is not what is."

"And you?" I asked, not believing any of that crap.

"I am an artificial construct put here to monitor the heavens,

78

welcome The One Who Comes and do some occasional cleaning and dusting to keep the area looking nice."

"So you're not real, either?"

"Nothing is what it appears, Alice Jane," the Krone said. "For example, we are not standing on the surface of a planet, as you probably imagine. We are actually on a rather large salvage ship traveling through the universe at near-light speed."

Okay, I didn't expect that.

"A big spaceship? Seriously?" I said.

"The mission of Eris—which is the name of this ship—is to scrounge for items of value and bring them back to sell, reuse or recycle."

"Back where?" I asked.

"Home," she said.

I was hoping for few more details.

"What kinds of 'items' are you talking about?" I said.

"Scrap, space garbage, valuable minerals, precious metals, stray comets, ideas, dreams, prophecies, planets and stars," she said. "Whatever looks interesting and might be worth something."

"How is that even possible?"

"Eris is hollow like a large ball," she said. "All of the 'samples,' as they are called, are compressed and then cataloged and stored until we return home."

"What kind of stupid mission is that?"

"A very lucrative one," she said. "Eris has been scavenging the universe for more than 5,000 years. There is already a world of riches inside its belly."

"You can't just steal stars and planets," I said. "I'm pretty sure there's a law about that."

"Interstellar law is ambiguous. There are no rules," she said. "And as long as nobody complains…."

It seemed illegal to me. Plus, people were dying. She didn't mention that part.

"What about all the soldiers here? Where do they fit in?"

"Seeded on Eris generations ago," she said. "They are inconsequential."

Of course they were.

"So whose ship is this?" I asked.

"Eris is owned by a multi-galactic holding corporation. PT Amalgamated Properties LLC, it is called," she said. "It is properly registered and licensed."

Gulp.

In case you didn't know, last year I negotiated Philbus Trot out of practically every corporation and business in the universe. PT Amalgamated Properties LLC was one of those companies. In other words, it was mine. (Before I died, that is.)

"So is Captain Tagg in charge of everything?" I asked.

"No. He takes orders from the Command Center," she said.

"And the fighting and the war?"

"That is not important," the Krone said.

Tell that to the injured and dying down below. And to Shem's parents.

"Okay, let's say I believe you," I said. (Which I didn't.) "What do you do around here? You said monitoring and greeting and cleaning up. For five millennia?"

"I serve as a sentry or watchman," the Krone said.

"So what have you seen and learned?" I asked, curious.

She closed her eyes.

"There is a great dread in the universe," the Krone said.

I could have told her that after standing in the middle of Dorkville, Minnesota, for five minutes.

"A sense of enormous loss and unimaginable grief," the Krone continued.

"Can you translate that into English?" I asked.

"I will show you something instead," the Krone said. "Words that will guide you in your journey."

She handed me a slip of what seemed like ancient papyrus, with three sentences that could have been written thousands of years ago. Or yesterday. Which they probably were.

I read:

I am here.
I am a broken heart.
I am the cry of a lonely soul.

"I don't get it," I said.

"It's sad, Alice Jane," Shem said.

I got that part.

Okay, this was not going well. Solving a confusing word puzzle and starting a crazy journey were not part of my plan. And that poem or song or whatever it was, what did it even mean? Who was this "I" and where was "here"? And the rest of it? The "broken heart" and the "cry of a lonely soul"? In my opinion, whoever wrote those sixteen words needed a whole team of psycho doctors, not Alice Jane Zelinski.

"So what happens if I don't solve this puzzle or go on this journey?" I asked.

"Three days remain," she said.

"Until what?"

"The End," she said.

15

A Long Shot

"You *know* this…person?" Jot asked as I stood in the clearing clutching the big leather book and listening to the deafening voices of the one thousand chanting priests of The Holy Order of The Healer.

"Philbus Trot," I said with a sigh. "Yeah."

"I don't believe I have had the pleasure," he said to Jot with a bow. "I am former Ambassador—and intergalactic superstar—Philbus Trot. And, if truth be told, I am also one of the ten most eligible bachelors in the cosmos, according to *Best Looking People Everywhere* magazine."

He winked. Twice.

"I know who you are," she said with a sour look.

Philbus Trot turned to me.

"Do you smell romance in the air, Wilkin?" he said in a sing-song voice.

"We're done, people," Jot said, spitting on the ground and vanishing down the trail with Reggie, Ozzie and the rest of her crew.

I wanted to get away, too.

"What are you doing here, Mr. Trot?" I asked.

"No need to thank me, Wilkin," he said. "I let it slip to my friends in The Holy Order"—he gestured toward the chanting, white-robed people—"that, along with being the 'Secret Weapon,' you are 'The Healer.' The one they've been seeking for thousands of years."

"Why would you do something like that?"

"To help an old friend, of course," he said with a big smile.

We were definitely not friends. Old or new.

As you probably know, Philbus Trot wiped out the dinosaurs, lost two moons, caused continental drift and nearly got us all killed when we closed the Fiz a few years ago. Plus there was the catastrophic incident known as "The Big Oops." (Conserving energy? Really?) And Jot said he'd destroyed half of a galaxy just getting to Eris.

He was a disaster.

"Tell me," I said, "can this sixteen word poem or whatever it is help me stop that black hole from killing us all?"

Philbus Trot leaned in close.

"It's not my area of expertise, Mr. Delgado," he said. "The Holy Order seems keen on the idea that the Sacred Words will somehow help you heal the universe. Personally, I don't put much stock in it. They're all a bit 'off,' if you want my professional opinion."

I shouldn't have asked.

"You never told me why you're on this planet," I said.

"'Planet,' did you call it?" he said with a smirk. "Eris used to be one of my many real estate holdings, you might say. Once I got word of your assignment—and the whole 'Secret Weapon' business—I came as quickly as I could to help you shut down that dangerous black hole and rescue the universe." He smiled. "I know this world intimately. And I thought you might be in need of an expert to guide you through its secret passages and into its many hidden places, including the secure Command Center. For a small finder's fee, of course."

Of course.

"I don't think I need your help," I said.

"Really, Mr. Delgado?" he said, straightening his necktie. "With a film crew following your every move, Cardie stuck in that miserable jail cell, Miss Zelinski deceased and that bothersome puffin gone AWOL? I would say you can use all the help you can get."

That stopped me cold.

"Wait a minute," I said. "Deceased? Alice Jane is dead?"

I was in shock.

"You didn't know?" he said, surprised. "Oh, dear. I hate to be the bearer of such terrible news. Found washed up on the Inside, I'm afraid. Not much left of her. We are all saddened by the loss, of course. In fact, I am now Chairman of the Alice Jane Zelinski Foundation, which is dedicated to serving humanitarian interests throughout the cosmos."

He handed me a business card that said exactly that. The card prominently featured a photo of his slimy, smiling face.

"I don't believe you," I said. "I just saw Alice Jane in Warrensberg a couple days ago."

"The official records are incontrovertible," he said. "Her cremated remains have already been returned to the Zelinski family."

The truth? I didn't think anyone or anything could kill Alice Jane Zelinski. Ever. I mean, in the three years I'd known her, she'd out tug-o-warred a Gutrog, held the universe together with her bare hands and survived a jolt of sixty septillion joules of electric current. Ordinary people can't do that.

"How did it happen?" I asked in a daze.

"I don't know the finer details," Philbus Trot said. "Her demise was quite a surprise to all of us. And the handbag and shoe manufacturers are still reeling, as you might have guessed. But we must carry on somehow. Miss Zelinski would have wanted it that way."

Alice Jane would have wanted to squash you like a cockroach, is what I was thinking.

"So what's this 'finder's fee' of yours all about?" I asked.

"Only what is—or was—rightfully mine," he said. "A small package. A few seeds. It's of no consequence."

That's when Sergeant Grimes, Digger, Sal, Loaf and Scuzz pushed their way through the throng of religious fanatics.

"You're a popular guy, Chief," Digger said. "Easy to find."

"And so inspirational," Sal said, squeezing my arm.

"You're a dirtball," Loaf said.

"Private Delgado, this is not a church or revival meeting," Grimes said. "Tell your religious friends to get off the premises so we can conduct official military business."

"They're not really my friends," I said.

"Allow me, Wilkin," Philbus Trot said, nudging me aside. He turned to The Holy Order and raised his hands, as if offering a universal blessing. "The Healer thanks you for your guidance, and pledges to deliver a transformed world within four days, in accordance with the prophecy. So go back to your caves and wait for the New Becoming."

The thousand robed figures bowed and then silently dispersed into the wilderness as if they were never there.

"I will return shortly, Wilkin," Philbus Trot told me confidentially. "I need to freshen up and gather my things."

Me? I rejoined the Happy Hippos.

My mind churned as we walked back to camp. I didn't know why I was on Eris or how I was supposed to heal the universe. And I couldn't get over the fact that Alice Jane was dead. Scuzz, on the other hand, didn't seem bothered by anything. He continued to sharpen his sword as he marched a couple of feet ahead of me.

"You ever hurt anyone with that?" I asked him.

He stopped and turned.

"No" Scuzz said with a feeble shake of his head.

He was young. Maybe eleven or twelve.

"Look," I said, "I'm scared, too."

That surprised him.

"But you're the Secret Weapon," he said.

"Everybody's scared," I said.

"My dad told me, 'Always keep a sharp blade,'" Scuzz said. "'And when it's time,' he said, 'don't think about it. Do it.'"

"You think you could kill?"

"I don't know," Scuzz said. "But I'll be ready."

Then he turned and ran to catch up with the rest of our unit.

Ten minutes later I was back in camp, still agonizing over what to do next. I sat on my blanket and hefted that oversized leather book onto my lap and skimmed the first of the Introductions. (Not helpful). Then I started reading the second Introduction, which was titled: "Theosophical Origins: The Words and Their Meanings." I skipped the first few paragraphs and read:

Over eons, serious scholars and even curious schoolchildren have wrestled with what is generally known as "The Sixteen Sacred Words of Eris," in an effort to uncover a hidden message or deeper meaning in the work. The most popular interpretation, espoused by The Holy Order of The Healer, is that this "sacred text" describes the arrival of a Healer or Redeemer who "comes from the stars to save a troubled world." Others suggest that the work presages a rebirth or reboot of the universe, and a second Big Bang. Some see it as a fragment of a larger work that has been mislaid or destroyed, and whose full meaning is therefore unknowable. It has also been called "a simple poem of questionable literary merit." And one rather unbalanced professor and part-time pastry chef even believes it to be a recipe for stew—a kind of jambalaya or bouillabaisse.

Stew?

I needed to do something to save the universe. But what? Cardamon Webb told me there was a connection between this crazy Flipside planet and the really black black hole. Trot said he knew the hidden secrets of Eris. And the poem? The Holy Order said it would help me heal everything.

I went back to "The Sixteen Sacred Words of Eris."

After rereading that frustrating poem for the ninety-seventh time, I got the impression it was telling me to go somewhere ("I am come") and speak honestly to someone ("I am an open heart") and hope that she or he had some big laser beam or supernova ("I am the light of a thousand suns") to stop the black hole from sucking us all inside. So right then I decided to get Philbus Trot to take me to the Command Center so I could talk to the person in charge and find out…something, anything…and try to fix the swirling, shrinking cosmos.

It was a long shot, but it was the best I could do.

I set down the book and left the tent to talk to the Happy Hippos.

"Sergeant Grimes," I said, "I have an idea how we can win the war."

16

A Cry for Help

"Look, lady," I said, "I think you got the wrong person."

As you know, I was standing on top of a 14,000-foot mountain on an illegal scavenging spaceship the size of a small planet, and talking to an "artificial construct" called the Krone. She said she'd been waiting for me for thousands of years, but since I'm a youthful (and svelte!) seventeen, her math was off big time. And her information was off-the-charts wrong, too. All I wanted was a good place to bury Jasper. That's it. (And maybe a just-out-of-the-oven cake doughnut with chocolate frosting and multi-colored sprinkles, if possible.) Was that too much to ask?

Apparently.

"It was the prophecy," the Krone said, her pink robes fluttering in the soft breeze.

"I'm not even supposed to be here," I said.

"Yet here you are."

Okay, she had a point.

"So what's the deal? What am I supposed to do?" I asked, holding the poem between my fingers and feeling a throbbing pain from my sore ribs.

"Our earliest records speak of a powerful warrior of exceptional beauty and wisdom who will hear the cry and save us all," she said.

That did sound a lot like me.

"And this poem, where did it come from?"

"It is written in the gaps and the emptiness, and on the dark matter of space," she said. "It is written on the smallest atom and the largest galaxy."

"Don't you think you're exaggerating just a little bit?"

I mean, what she was talking about was some kind of intergalactic All Points Bulletin. A literal cry for help to the universe. And it wasn't just a Post-it Note stuck on an interstellar refrigerator or sad country music radio waves flying around in the depths of outer space. It was a message imprinted on everything everywhere like a full body tattoo.

"We have to do something, Alice Jane," Shem said, tugging on my chain mail shirt.

Not necessarily.

"Who wrote it?" I asked.

"There is no signature," she said.

Of course.

"When was it written?" I asked. "And don't give me that crap about 5,000 years ago. I'm not buying that."

"It was recorded after all the parts and pieces of the universe joined together and then drifted apart," she said.

Huh?

"I think she's talking about the 'crumpling,' Alice Jane," Shem whispered.

That made sense. Or as much sense as any of the insane garbage that Krone lady was spewing at me.

"So what's the deal with this three-day countdown?" I asked.

"The convergence has returned," the Krone said. "We are spiraling toward a common point that will consume all things."

Couldn't she talk like a real person?

"You mean a black hole?" I said.

"Yes," the Krone replied.

My reconstructed earlobes tingled. So much for a soothing bath and a half-dozen cake doughnuts. This was serious.

"Let me go on record as saying that I'm here by accident," I said. "I just want to bury my friend, not go on some deadly journey and end up as roadkill on the Flipside. Understand?"

"It is your decision," the Krone said.

She was getting on my nerves.

"So what am I supposed to do?" I asked with a sigh.

"Follow me," she said.

As we walked in single file—the Krone, then me, Shem and Loretta, who was actually flying—across a narrow mountain pass, I took another look at the poem:

I am here.
I am a broken heart.
I am the cry of a lonely soul.

Stupid.

The Krone took us to a ledge that looked out on the hull of that planet-sized spaceship. She pointed to a tall red tower in the distance that rose from the surface and disappeared into the wispy clouds like a bridge to the end of the universe.

"Your journey will take you there," she said.

It was a long way away. And a long way to the top.

"And then what?"

"You will know," she said.

Of course.

I was just about ready to say, "Thanks, but no thanks," but instead I leaned my head back and watched as planets and star systems moved across the sky like they were caught in an enormous cosmic undertow. That's when I knew everything she'd told me was true. (Especially the part about the "powerful warrior of exceptional beauty and wisdom.") But what could I do to stop a universe that was spiraling out of control?

It was the first time I actually wished I could talk to Cardamon Webb.

"Loretta," I said, "what are we supposed to do? How do we stop the universe from getting sucked in on itself? What does that poem even mean?"

Loretta stared at me long and hard.

"I'm just a bird," she said.

Not helpful.

We left the Krone on that ledge. Her job was done, and ours was just beginning. (Again.)

As we descended the mountain, I stared at Shem. She was calm and seemed almost happy.

"Why aren't you scared out of your skivvies right now?" I asked her.

She looked up at me.

"Because I'm with you, Alice Jane," Shem said.

She had a good point.

17

Lies

I lied.

I didn't have a clue how to win the war. And, to be truthful, I didn't care. I just wanted to get to the Command Center on Eris, talk to whoever was in charge about the black hole, and stop the deadly spiraling of the cosmos. It wasn't much of a plan. After all, my information was sketchy: Instructions from an imprisoned intergalactic plumber, a confusing ancient prophecy, an unrhyming sixteen word poem "of questionable literary merit," and the promises of a smarmy former Ambassador who wanted a "finder's fee" for his help.

"I know somebody who can sneak us across the FEBA and beyond enemy territory to the Command Center," I told Grimes. "Once there, we can take it over and declare victory."

"You're serious?" he asked.

"I'm sure it'll work," I said. (Lying again.)

"How do we find this Command Center?" Grimes asked suspiciously.

"My, uh, friend. He knows," I said. "Former Ambassador

Philbus Trot. He used to live here, I think."

"Hm. I like the idea of doing something, instead of just sitting," Grimes said, absentmindedly splitting a table in half with his axe.

"And we've got the Secret Weapon," Digger said, pointing a "thumb" at me. "No doubt about that. Right, Chief?"

"Right," I said. (Lying for a third time.)

"Sal?" Grimes said.

"Beats being killed on the battlefield," she said.

"Agreed. I'll check with the higher-ups and see if we can get a go-ahead," Grimes said, walking off in the direction of the headquarters building.

We spent the rest of the day packing our backpacks and sharpening our weapons, preparing to leave as soon as we got orders to move. The big leather book took up most of the room in my pack, which meant I only had enough extra space for toothpaste and a toothbrush.

When Jot and the film crew arrived, they were surprised to see us almost ready to go.

"What's happening?" Jot asked.

"Secret mission. Hush-hush stuff," Sal said, stuffing a dozen maps and an assortment of guidebooks into her pack.

"We're sneaking into the Command Center so we can take it down and claim victory," Loaf said. "Stupid plan."

"Why wasn't I informed?" Jot asked. "I'm part of this unit, you know."

"Talk to our Secret Weapon," Loaf said. "It's his idiotic idea."

Jot scowled and then pulled me aside.

"We're a team, Wilkin. You have to keep me in loop," she said. "You weren't planning to leave me here, I hope."

"Of course not," I said. (Lying yet again.)

"Reggie, Ozzie, get everything packed up and ready to go," Jot said. "We're bugging out of here."

Minutes later, Grimes returned with a signed authorization in his hand and something that resembled a smile on his face.

"It's a 'Go.' HQ is all for it," he said. "We leave at nightfall."

That's when Philbus Trot and eight of the white-robed religious fanatics crashed through the bushes and overran our camp. The priests struggled under the weight of five large trunks, fourteen suitcases, eleven garment bags and seven baskets of dirty laundry.

"Sorry I'm late, everyone," Philbus Trot said, carrying only his thin leather briefcase. "It took hours to get my things together for our little adventure."

"This is your friend?" Grimes asked me.

I nodded. (Lie.)

"It's a big mistake, Sergeant," Jot said to Grimes. "Mr. Trot is widely known and has a certain…reputation. It's not good."

"And he doesn't pack light, either," Sal said.

"I don't care if he clucks like a chicken, Miss Tropacana," Grimes said. "As long as the former Ambassador can take us to this Command Center and help us win the war, he can do whatever he wants."

After the suns set on the seven horizons, Reggie got his camera and microphone into position to document the Happy Hippos leaving on our dangerous and secret mission, which was apparently being broadcast live to twenty-seven billion people. Maybe more.

Some secret.

"Mr. Delgado and I will take the lead, of course," Philbus Trot said. "The rest of you try to keep up as best you can."

"Sword in the air, Wilkin. And chin up," Jot said encouragingly. "Remember: Grim determination."

94

I unsheathed my duct taped sword, which gave me a painful shock, and then raised it high over my head. It was a lot lighter than the "fearless" sword, but my arm still got tired, so I ended up dragging it in the dirt as I walked along, leaving a trail of blue sparks behind me. I hoped my fear and uncertainty translated into "grim determination" on TV.

"Let's move," Grimes said. "And try to stay together."

We walked more than a dozen miles along rocky trails and past scarred hills. As we got nearer to the battlefield, the sounds of war grew louder: Blasts and cries, nightmarish screams and shouts. Clouds of smoke and dust surrounded us. And the smell of burning plastic and singed flesh filled our nostrils.

At one point the smoke cleared, and we came upon another wave of soldiers prepared to enter the battle and sacrifice their lives.

"People, people, put down your weapons," Philbus Trot told them. "Kick back and let the Secret Weapon do his job."

Then the coarse black smoke swallowed everything up again.

"Mr. Former Ambassador, we're still at war. Do that again and I'll chop you up into hamburger," Grimes said.

"Just trying to be helpful," Philbus Trot said.

We kept moving.

"Where are we going?" I asked Philbus Trot.

"The entire 'planet,' if you will, is crisscrossed with a network of ducts to transport heat and fresh air to the surface," he said. "I know where there's a rather large hole in one of the vents not far from here. The result of stray mortar fire, I believe. It's like a big open door. We can walk right through."

That seemed too easy.

"You're not telling me something," I said.

"Just rumors," he said. "Not to worry."

"Rumors?"

"So-called 'tunnel rats,'" Philbus Trot said dismissively.

"Rats?"

"They're people. The poor souls retreated from the surface and now live in the ducts like rats in the sewers," Philbus Trot said. "It's most depressing. And unsanitary."

"Are these tunnel rats dangerous?"

"Maybe. Probably not. Actually, I don't concern myself with such minor details," Philbus Trot said. "We must keep a positive outlook in all things, as you know."

I was almost ready to panic and run, but I was stuck. I didn't have a backup plan. None. And (unfortunately) the plan I did have depended on the most self-centered, deceitful and foolish person in the universe.

In other words, we were doomed.

"So what's in all these suitcases and trunks?" I asked.

"I am prepared for any emergency," Philbus Trot said, taking a small mirror from his suit coat pocket and checking his teeth, eyebrows and profile. Satisfied, he returned the mirror to his pocket.

"Like an attack of tunnel rats, for example?" I asked hopefully.

"Please, Wilkin, be serious," he said. "In our quest, there is the off chance we will meet up with certain dignitaries and distinguished heads-of-state." I stared at him in disbelief. "I must have the proper attire," he added.

"It's a bunch of clothes?"

"According to my somewhat conservative calculations, I may need to attend as many as 121 possible formal or official events on this trip," Philbus Trot said. "You can rest assured that I am prepared for every one of them."

"One hundred and twenty-one suits?"

"Plus a dozen or so robes, sport coats and exercise outfits. And shirts, socks, belts, ties and shoes, of course," he said. "I need to consider all the potential variations. From state dinners to yacht cruises to stress-relieving meetings at a luxurious spa or hot spring."

Philbus Trot was bonkers.

We walked for another half hour until we came to a place of craters and broken rock. Half of a mountain had been ripped apart, exposing a thick plastic pipe five stories tall with a hole in the side as big as a pregnant elephant.

"This is the entrance I mentioned," Philbus Trot said. "I've used it once or twice before."

"That's good intel, Mr. Former Ambassador," Grimes said as he climbed up to study the damaged duct.

"What are we waiting for?" Sal said, eager to get inside.

"Last rites, I think," Loaf said.

"Gotta follow the Secret Weapon," Digger said. "Right, Chief?"

Right.

"Get a good shot of this, Reggie," Jot said. And to me she added, "Wilkin, get in front of the opening. Look like you're leading the charge." And to the rest of the group she shouted, "Everybody else, get behind Wilkin. Moon eyes, people, moon eyes. Act as if he's your hero leading you to victory."

"Or death," Loaf said.

A short time later we managed to squeeze all of us and the trunks and luggage and dirty laundry through the blast hole. Sensors apparently recognized our presence and lit the long corridor, which was silent and empty.

Mostly.

Right away I tripped over something big and brown and smelly.

97

"Looks like rat poop," Loaf said, kicking a couple of the droppings, which were the size of large zucchinis.

"That right, Mr. Former Ambassador?" Grimes asked, raising his axe as he looked in both directions for signs of danger.

"There may be a few stray vermin—and other not-so-friendly creatures," he said.

"I don't like the looks of it," Sal said.

"We'll be fine," I said. (Really big lie.)

18

Scrubbers

A bird, a kid, a left leg, a poem and yours truly. That was pretty much our entire Saving the Universe Team. And, believe it or not, I didn't like our chances. I mean, it was obvious we didn't have a clue how to stop the "convergence," or whatever you want to call it. Plus, our instructions were a bit vague. "Get to the top of the tower," the Krone had told me. *And then?* "You will know," she said. *Anything else?* "You only have three days," she added. *Thanks.*

We were toast.

As we climbed down the mountain, with the tall red tower looming in the distance, I watched Shem leap from rock to rock. She'd come a long way from that annoying girl selling battle armor in the middle of a muddy swamp. She was more relaxed. More like a normal nine- or ten-year-old. After about an hour we took a break, drank some water, chewed on a few sprouts and relaxed, while Loretta flew away to locate the tower entrance.

"I need a serious raise," Shem's left leg said, flopping onto a big rock and breathing hard.

"It's not used to so much walking," Shem said, as her leg ran off to stretch and roll on the rugged ground. "The altitude doesn't help, either."

"So what's your story?" I asked, loosening my armor. "You said your parents were attacked on the Field of Blood. Were they soldiers?"

She shook her head slowly.

"When everything was crumpling—and the world was dying—we were scared like everybody else," she said. "The Holy Order, they said it's what we deserved, and told us about a New Becoming."

"Sounds like some kind of religious cult," I said.

"They said the world was ending because of all the hatred and meanness, and because we didn't believe," Shem said. "They said a few 'chosen' people would be lifted up or transformed—like gods."

"And they were serious?"

"Everybody expected the world to end, Alice Jane," she said. "The priests told us we had to climb to the top of the mountain, and after everything crumpled we'd become something new and special and timeless, and live among the stars."

"That's stupid," I said, because it was.

"I guess," Shem said. "But we didn't have much. Just the store and ourselves. And when we looked at all the planets and suns and galaxies crashing into each other, it was like we didn't have a choice. We were going to die anyway. And what if…?"

Okay, that made sense in some crazy, End of Everything way.

"So you and your parents decided to cross the battlefield," I said.

"They didn't make it," Shem said quietly. "And after…I couldn't carry them. They were too heavy. And there was blood."

100

Her eyes filled with tears. "So I dragged them, or what was left. I wanted to bring them up here. But when I was almost to the other side, there was a giant explosion." She stared blankly into the distance. "Someone found us and brought us back. They gave me my prosthesis. And the shoeboxes with my mom and dad." She bit her lower lip. "I'm almost like new, Alice Jane. I don't notice having one leg most of the time." She looked at the emptiness where her leg used to be. "Sometimes it's better than before."

"'Harmony of mind and body,' as Master Woo would say," I said.

"Is that good?" she asked hungrily.

"It's perfect," I said.

Shem grinned.

"What happened then?" I asked.

"When the crumpling was over, I went back to the store and sat around and watched TV," Shem said. "Mostly about the Secret Weapon."

"What's that?"

"It was all over the news," Shem said. "Some boy from another world who's supposed to end the war."

Wilkin?

"I think I know who you mean," I said.

And good luck with that.

"Alice Jane, when I saw you walk into the shop with your skin all alive and swirly—and that eye tattoo on the back of your neck—I thought you were the Secret Weapon for real."

"That's a bunch of crap," I said.

"You got that right," her left leg said, leaping into the air and then reattaching itself to Shem's stump.

Shem laughed and we got up and continued our descent.

Progress was slow and the tower seemed like it was getting

farther away. Plus the stars and planets were uncomfortably close and bright, which made it hard to tell if it was day or night. After six or seven hours, we found a place with soft moss-like undergrowth, dense purple bushes, level ground and a couple of overhanging rocks for shade. As we set up camp, Shem stared at my face.

"Alice Jane," she said, "what happens when you bleed?"

"What kind of sick question is that?"

"All those squiggles and shapes under your skin," she said, touching the back of my hand. "If you cut yourself, do they come out?"

"They're deeper than that. Locked inside. I don't know how," I said.

We gnawed on a few sprouts and prepared for sleep. Shem's left leg crept into the bushes and disappeared. Shem dropped off a few seconds later. I closed my eyes and made my own night, dreaming of black holes and sad poems.

After a few hours, we were startled awake by Shem's left leg shouting, "Keep back. I'm warning you!"

I grabbed my Iknatian spear and got into a forward stance.

"What is it?" I hissed.

"Scrubber," Shem's left leg said. "Mean one."

What?

"I got it," Shem said with a lazy yawn.

She sat up and let her leg attach itself to her stump, then she grabbed a small dagger from her belt and crawled silently across the ground and into the bushes. Not long after that, there was a scraping and a screech, and Shem reappeared holding something that looked like a cross between a Snickers candy bar and a hairbrush. It had a brown, box-like, rubbery body with thousands of little black hairy mechanical "legs" that wiggled and whirred.

Shem prodded the Scrubber with her dagger a couple of times. It gave a mechanical belch, stopped moving and all of its dozen small lights blinked out.

"We get these things at the shop every once in a while," Shem said. "I think they clean the air and water, add stuff to the soil, check the weather and keep things neat and tidy. We call them Scrubbers."

I took the spiky bot from Shem and turned it over in my hands. It had sensors and lights and legs and probes.

"Does it do things on its own or does someone control it?" I asked.

"I'm not sure. But I think they're all connected," Shem said. "Last summer I found one that was bent up and crushed. I cleaned it off, painted it red, put it back together and started it up again. I even added racing stripes and a Twitter account. And named it Zippy."

Zippy?

"What happened?"

"In about twenty-five minutes there were like thirty or forty of them all around the shop," Shem said. "I tossed Zippy out the window and never saw her again."

My mom would've loved a couple of Scrubbers to clean the house. And I could picture Genghis playing cat and mouse with one of them, too. Imagining that made me think about home. I'd only been gone a few days, but I missed just about everything. Even crappy Warrensberg.

That's when I heard a chorus of ear-splitting metallic squeals and grindings that sounded like a cage fight between a circular saw and a garbage disposal. I crouched low and moved silently in a circle, slicing the air with my Iknatian spear.

Then I gulped.

We were not alone.

The entire mountain was covered with Scrubbers. Lots of them.

"There must be thousands. Millions. I've never seen so many," Shem said.

She gulped, too.

"And they're not happy," I said.

19

Mission Trip

We entered the air duct through the blast hole, turned left and walked for several miles down a long tunnel that was like a giant hamster tube. There were no "You Are Here" signs, so we didn't know our exact location, but the eighteen of us (plus Trot's luggage) were able to make good time on our way to the Command Center.

"I believe the enemy camp is directly above us," Philbus Trot said.

"That's what I see on the map," Sal said.

"Do we need to be quiet?" Ozzie asked.

"Too far down," Jot said. "We're at least half a mile beneath the surface."

When we stopped to rest, the only sounds came from our breathing, the constant scraping of Scuzz sharpening his sword and the faint whistle of warm, fresh air moving through the duct.

"Think there's a Fanta machine down here, Chief?" Digger asked.

I shook my head.

A few miles later, we entered a large room that split off in about twenty different directions.

"Which way, Mr. Former Ambassador?" Grimes said.

"It's one of these," Philbus Trot said, gesturing toward a dozen of the openings.

That's when the lights went out.

"I can't see my knees," Digger said.

"Reggie, use the camera lights," Jot said.

Reggie's camera lit the immediate area around our group. (Including Digger's knees.) Beyond that, everything disappeared in shadows and darkness.

"That's as good as it gets," Reggie said.

Next we heard a scuffing of feet and the jostling of bodies nearby. We huddled together and prepared for a fight. As I withdrew my sword, it gave me a huge electric shock, and I nearly chopped off Loaf's ear.

"Who's out there?" Grimes shouted.

His voice echoed in twenty different directions.

Then the lights came back on and I blinked and shielded my eyes.

We were surrounded by an army of more than a hundred scrawny men and women dressed in rags and holding swords, knives, maces, axes, sticks, wrenches and shovels pointed in our direction.

Tunnel rats.

"Put down your weapons," Rat #1 told us.

I dropped my sword, which sent sparks in every direction. That was followed by clanging and a few yelps as the axes and swords of the others fell onto the floor or landed on unprotected toes.

"Give me one good reason we shouldn't kill you now," Rat

#2 said.

"We don't want to die," Digger said. "Is that a good enough reason?"

Rats #3, #4 and #5 all shook their heads.

"I am Philbus Trot," the former Ambassador said. "Intergalactic superstar."

Silence.

"That's the best you can come up with?" Rat #6 said finally.

"This would be a good time to do a Secret Weapony thing, Chief," Digger whispered to me.

Like what?

"Hi, I'm Wilkin Delgado," I said uncertainly, trying to come up with a plan that wouldn't get us all killed. "So...do you folks live around here?"

They looked at me like I was insane.

"To quote Emily Dickinson," Rat #7 said, "'Where thou art, that is home.'"

"We art here, so the answer is 'Yes,'" Rat #8 said.

What do you say when someone starts quoting Emily Dickinson?

"They're probably spies," Rat #9 said.

"We're not spies. And we don't want to hurt anybody," I said. "We come in peace."

"Then why the weapons?" Rat #10 said.

Good question.

"We heard there were...rats," I said.

"That's us," Rat #11 said. "They call us 'tunnel rats.' Not very flattering. But as we all know, 'Beauty is not in the face; beauty is a light in the heart.'"

"Khalil Gibran," Rat #12 said. "Well said."

This was not going well.

"*You're* the tunnel rats?" I said, trying to sound surprised and happy. (I was neither.) "We've been looking all over for you!"

"I find that hard to believe," Rat #13 said.

"Nobody wants to see us," Rat #14 said. "Not even us."

They laughed.

"Can we kill them now?" Rat #15 asked.

My mind raced. What could we do? How could we escape? I mean, we had nothing. No valuables. (Unless you count the ancient leather book with the sixteen word poem.) No information to barter with. (Except that the universe was going to be squished to the size of a gnat's brain in three days and counting.) And no reason to be in the tunnels. (Except to go to the Command Center and talk to the person in charge and figure out how to keep the cosmos from flushing itself to death.) Plus we had Philbus Trot and his luggage and dirty laundry, which was a colossal waste.

Or was it?

"We…represent the Alice Jane Zelinski Foundation," I said. "We're on a mission trip to provide humanitarian aid to the tunnel rats of Eris." I smiled. "That's you."

They laughed again.

"Are you for real?" Rat #16 said.

"In all the years we've been down here," Rat #17 said, poking me with the point of his very sharp dagger, "that's the first we've heard of 'humanitarian aid.'"

"Nobody cares about us," Rat #14 said. "Not even us."

"I'm serious," I said, even though I was lying through my teeth.

"Let him speak," Rat #18 said. "As Martin Luther King, Jr., said, 'Life's most persistent and urgent question is, "What are you doing for others?"' So it could be he's telling the truth."

"Yes, but let's not forget Aristotle," Rat #19 said. "'Happiness belongs to the self sufficient.' In other words, we probably don't need whatever it is they have. And even if we did, we might as well kill them anyway."

"I don't think that's what Aristotle had in mind," I said nervously.

"Now the Dalai Lama…," Rat #20 began.

"That's enough. Let's hear their little spiel and then we'll kill them," Rat #21 said. "We can use the entertainment. Not much to do around here except read and argue."

I swallowed hard.

"What I'm telling you is true. We're official and everything. Here's our card," I said, digging into my pocket and locating Philbus Trot's business card.

"Philbus Trot, huh?" Rat #22 said, looking at the photo and then at the real thing. "That's you?"

"The photo doesn't do me justice, as you can see," Philbus Trot said, smoothing his eyebrows.

"Says here your Foundation is 'dedicated to serving humanitarian interests throughout the cosmos.' Is that right?" Rat #22 asked our group.

All eighteen heads nodded in agreement.

"Wait a minute," Rat #23 said, "I've heard of this Alice Jane Zelinski. She's the doughnut lady. The one who put in all those gift shops."

"I like her," Rat #24 said.

"So do I," Rat #25 said.

"And that pink galaxy, that was hers, too," Rat #26 said.

There was a buzz of excitement.

I couldn't believe it. Alice Jane was more popular in an underground air duct on the edge of the Flipside than she was in her own home back on Earth.

"I heard she tricked some idiot out of half the universe," Rat #27 said, chuckling.

"That's not really what…," Philbus Trot said.

"She's dead," I interrupted. "So we're carrying on her humanitarian mission."

"Dead, huh?" Rat #28 said. "So what do you have in those bags and cases? Doughnuts?"

"'Ich bin ein Berliner,'" Rat #29 said. "As John F. Kennedy said."

"They're much-needed humanitarian gifts," I said unconvincingly. "So we'll just leave them with you and be on our way, if that's okay."

"Open them up," Rat #30 said.

The tunnel rats broke open the trunks and suitcases. Inside they found layer after layer of cleaned and pressed wool dress suits. Size forty-two long.

"Be careful," Philbus Trot said. "They're worth more than 150,000 Slurbish rodondos each."

"They smell good, too," Rat #31 said, pressing his nose to the fabric.

"Suits? That's your humanitarian mission?" Rat #32 said disbelievingly.

I swallowed even harder.

"We, um, heard you were down here living in terrible conditions with only rags to wear," I said. "We thought you might like something more stylish. Make you feel better about yourselves. Go out on the town, maybe. 'Clothes make the man— and woman,' as somebody whose name I don't know once said."

Hey, I was doing my best.

"That's the stupidest thing I've ever heard," Rat #33 said.

"He's lying," Rat #34 said.

"Let's kill them," Rat #35 said.

"Wait. You're making a mistake," I said.

"Prove it," Rat #36 said challengingly.

"Um," I began in desperation, "what other possible reason could there be for us to bring 121 brand new wool suits into this air duct?"

Pause.

"Can't think of a one," Rat #37 said.

"He makes a good point," Rat #38 said.

"You know what Ernest Hemingway said," Rat #39 said.

In unison, all of the tunnel rats said, "'The best way to find out if you can trust somebody is to trust them.'"

All of the rats removed their ratty clothing and put on the suits, complete with white button-down cotton shirts, leather shoes, black socks, belts and colorful silk neckties.

"Don't we look nice," Rat #40 said.

And they did.

"Okay, let's say we believe you," Rat #41 said, looking at his spiffy reflection in the shiny sides of the tunnel.

"Thank you," I said.

"Don't get ahead of yourself, Mr. Wilkin Delgado," Rat #42 said. "Tell me, who are *they*?"

He pointed to the eight priests of The Holy Order

"Them? They're, um, priests," I said. "They're part of our holistic humanitarian assistance program. You see, we outfit you with a new look for your outside and at the same time support your internal spiritual needs. Full service."

"Uh-huh," he said. "And them?"

He pointed to Jot, Reggie and Ozzie.

"Documentary filmmakers," I said. "They're making a movie about the Alice Jane Zelinski Foundation. We're thinking IMAX."

"That true?" he asked Jot, Reggie and Ozzie.

They nodded vigorously.

"Either you're the biggest liars on this pitiful world, or the most misguided and charitable fools in the universe," he said. "Either way, we should probably kill all of you."

"I hope you'll reconsider," I said. "This is our first mission trip. We're just getting started."

"I like the suits," Rat #43 said.

"Wish they would have brought doughnuts, though," Rat #44 said.

"Okay, get out of here. All of you," Rat #45 said.

"Um, which way is the Command Center?" I asked as we quickly retrieved our weapons and scurried toward the twenty tunnels.

Rat #46 pointed to an opening on our right.

We ran.

20

Ping!

Another bad day in outer space.

Just as we were ready to hike the rest of the way down the mountain and climb the tall red tower to try to save everybody and everything, about a million Scrubbers swarmed around us and squeaked and blinked and threatened us with their little black legs. It was like being attacked by an army of angry bristle brushes.

Shem and I looked at each other.

"I think they're mad about the one I deactivated," Shem said.

"Can you turn it back on?"

"I think so."

I carefully handed Shem the disabled Scrubber and watched as she used a small knife to open a hidden panel in the bot's underside and flip a tiny switch and press a reset button.

We crossed our fingers.

In less than a minute, the bot's lights came on and it buzzed and bleeped happily in Shem's hands. She set it on the ground and we watched it scurry away to join its friends.

We both sighed.

And then we didn't.

"They're not leaving," I said, looking in every direction.

"I didn't do anything, Alice Jane," Shem said nervously.

"It's not you, it's them," I said. "They're still pissed off about something."

As you know, I'm a pretty good judge of when somebody or something is pissed off. (Especially me.) Those bots were crabby and on edge, and they looked like they wanted to kill something. (Probably us.) So I thought it best to try to get away as fast as we could. I took a tentative step forward and gently redirected several Scrubbers with the side of my boot.

"Okay, little bots," I said in my cheeriest voice. "We just want to get through. Clear the way. We're your friends."

It didn't work.

About twenty of them attacked my boot, ripping it apart with their sharp, articulated legs and probes. They tore big chunks out of the leather and almost reached my (formerly) perfectly pedicured tootsies. I wanted to skewer all of them with my spear, but instead I peeled off the offending Scrubbers one at a time and gently tossed them twenty-five or more feet away like I was skipping stones on a lake.

Not a good idea.

After that, there was a collective screech and instead of retreating, they surged toward us and piled on top of each other so I was buried in Scrubbers all the way up to my neck. I lifted Shem onto my shoulders, and she put her left leg on top of her head so we looked like a sad and sorry totem pole.

We needed a plan. A good one.

"You said they clean things?" I asked.

"That's what somebody told me," Shem said. "We'll be okay, won't we? They don't have mouths or teeth."

"They don't need them," I said, feeling my big toe poking through the shredded leather of my boot.

I had to think.

Our options were definitely limited. We couldn't run or even move. There were too many to fight. They didn't eat, sleep or go to the bathroom, so we couldn't outlast them. And they were mad. Even with my astounding good looks and Certificate of Completion from the Peace and Power Martial Arts Academy, the two of us were no match for a million grouchy Scrubbers.

"Maybe we can talk to them," Shem said.

"Do you speak Scrubber?" I asked.

She shook her head.

I searched the sky for Loretta.

Nothing.

So we waited.

After an hour or so, I noticed something in the valley moving toward us through the mass of Scrubbers. It was like a deer making its way through a Minnesota cornfield.

"Something's coming," I said, nodding my head toward the movement in the distance.

"What is it?" Shem asked.

"Probably a funeral director," Shem's left leg said.

Three interminable hours later (without a bathroom break, I might add), that endless carpet of bots parted in front of us, and out popped a cherry red Scrubber with white racing stripes.

I looked at Shem.

"Is that…?" I asked.

"Zippy," she said, brightening.

I heard a "Ping!" coming from Shem's pocket.

"It's…," Shem began.

"A tweet," I said. "I know."

She looked at her phone, then at me.

"Zippy says, 'Hey.'"

Ping!

"Now what?" I asked.

"It's a smiley face," Shem said.

Argh.

I wasn't in the mood to play games or catch up on old times. We needed to get out of there. Alive, if possible.

"Ask her if they'll let us go," I said.

Shem texted a message.

Ping!

"Well?"

"It's another smiley face."

Of course it was.

"Tell her we just want to get to the top of the tower and save the universe from spiraling into a black hole," I said. "And that we're running out of time."

Shem texted another message.

Ping!

"Well?" I asked.

"It's a selfie," Shem said, showing me a close-up image of Zippy's "face."

I tightened my grip on the Iknatian spear. I was ready to make shish kebab out of that bot.

"We need to get out of here," I said.

"Zippy's kind of excited," Shem said.

"*Amituofo. Amituofo. Amituofo,*" I grumbled, grinding my teeth and trying to center myself at the same time.

"What does that mean?" Shem asked.

"Find out if they're going to kill us," I said.

"I'll try."

Shem texted the message. And added a smiley face.

Ping!

"Well?"

"Zippy says they'll help us get to the tower," Shem said.

"Good answer," I said.

"They have one condition, though," Shem said. "Three, actually."

I didn't like the sound of that.

"Which are?"

"They all want paint jobs and racing stripes," Shem said. "And Twitter accounts."

21

Black Holes

We were lucky.

We'd miraculously escaped from an army of more than a hundred scruffy, homeless, disaffected, well-read and well-dressed tunnel rats, and were on our way to the Eris Command Center. Getting there was still going to be difficult (or impossible), but at least we didn't have to drag along the thirty pieces of Philbus Trot's luggage (plus seven baskets of his dirty laundry) or worry about another uncomfortable encounter with the tunnel rats (I hoped).

"Private Delgado," Grimes said, "good work back there."

"Thanks, Sergeant," I said.

"Most of the credit should be mine, of course," Philbus Trot said, tugging at his lapels. "After all, it was my impeccably tailored 100% worsted wool spring collection that allowed us to outwit those wretched hooligans."

Us?

"You getting any of this, Reggie?" Jot said. "Especially the fantastical delusions and egomania?"

"Every word," Reggie said.

"We're still stuck in this stinking tunnel," Loaf said.

"But we're alive," Sal said. "Wilkin was so brave, don't you think?"

"He's got a head on his shoulders, that's for sure," Digger said. "Right, Chief?"

We turned the corner and entered a much narrower air duct. From then on, I had to walk bent over so I didn't bump my aforementioned still-on-the-shoulders head. Looking down, I saw a few more of those big, stinky droppings. It wasn't a good sign.

"Where exactly are we, Mr. Former Ambassador?" Grimes asked.

"I don't have a detailed schematic on me at the moment, I'm afraid," Philbus Trot said, patting his pockets.

Sal held a five-inch stack of maps in front of his face.

"I got lots to choose from," she said.

Sal spread the largest of the maps onto the floor. All eighteen of us leaned in close, studying the lines and dots and roads and topography.

"Near as I can tell, the opening of that busted vent was here," Sal said, indicating a spot near the center of the map. "We've been headed in this direction for about five miles, maybe six. That would put us somewhere around here." She dropped a fingertip onto the upper corner of the map. "According to Mr. Trot, the Command Center is somewhere over here." She pointed to a spot on the floor that was about a foot and a half off the map.

We still had a long way to go and not much time left, so we picked up our belongings and kept moving.

Along the way, I tried to figure out the poem. It still didn't make any sense. How could those sixteen words possibly save the

119

cosmos from oblivion? And what did it have to do with me?

I am come.
I am an open heart.
I am the light of a thousand suns.

If I really was The Healer of The Holy Order's prophecy, then "I am come" might be short for "I am come from Warrensberg to save the universe from destruction." (Hey, it's possible.) But what about the "open heart"? Was it saying that my heart was filled with enough compassion and unconditional love to save humanity and everything else? (Probably not.) And let's not forget "the light of a thousand suns." Was I supposed to trigger a giant explosion of light that would somehow put the universe back in balance? (Maybe.)

I was confused.

"Mr. Trot," I said, "what can you tell me about black holes?"

"Practically everything, Mr. Delgado," he said, flashing one of his snarky smiles. "I can take them apart and put them back together blindfolded, if that's what you mean."

And destroy everything and everybody in the process, I said to myself.

"Okay, so how do you stop one from wrecking the universe?" I asked.

"The simple answer?" he asked. I nodded. "An equally powerful force," he answered.

"You mean like in Newton's First Law?"

"That's the general idea," he said.

I thought back to what my third grade teacher Ms. Jasperson taught me about Isaac Newton's Three Laws of Motion. The First Law is that objects at rest will stay at rest, and moving objects will keep moving unless they come up against an outside force.

"So what you're saying is we could take another super strong black hole and set the two against each other and stop the out-of-control spiraling and save us all?" I said hopefully.

Philbus Trot shook his head.

"If it were that simple, we'd be sipping tea and eating scones right now, Mr. Delgado," he said.

"But don't you use black holes to fix things?"

"On a much smaller scale," he said condescendingly. "In my professional opinion, the universe as we know it will be gone in a few days."

Thanks for the pep talk.

"So why even go to the Command Center?"

"I like to keep my options open," Philbus Trot said. "I'm also looking for a lost…something. The Seeds of Slebe."

"Is that the 'finder's fee' you mentioned?"

"It is said they can grow almost anything—including a new universe," he said.

Like I believed that.

We entered a large, bright room, set down our packs, drank some water and checked the map. Our group was quiet and contemplative.

Then somebody or something in the far corner cleared its throat and said, "Welcome."

22

A Long Way Up

I did the math.

Let's say there were a million Scrubbers and that it'd take thirty minutes to paint and decorate each one. That's 500,000 hours or a little more than fifty-seven years working twenty-four hours a day to spruce up all those little bots. And that didn't include coffee breaks, sleep or carpal tunnel surgeries. Or the tens of thousands of hours needed to set up a million Twitter accounts.

In other words, it was impossible.

"Tell them, 'No problem,'" I said to Shem.

Look, I'm all about keeping my word. (As you know.) But I didn't have a lot of options. For one thing, I was practically a prisoner surrounded by all those pissed off bots, and there was a good chance I'd die waiting for them to get bored or for help to arrive. And it's not like they were people. I mean, a promise to a mechanical scrub brush is a whole lot different than a promise to a gastropod mollusk, Blop, Zorazeen or human, right? Plus there was a good chance we (and the rest of the universe) wouldn't live long enough for any of it to matter. So it was probably a moot point anyway.

Shem texted the message.

There was a pause, and then the entire mountain erupted in happy bleeps and whirs.

Ping!

"Zippy says it's a deal," Shem said.

"You might want to mention that first we have to get to the top of the tower and save the universe," I said.

"And that we might die trying," Shem's left leg added.

Shem texted the message.

Ping!

"It's another smiley face, Alice Jane," Shem said. "And they'll help us get down the mountain, too."

I didn't want any help. I just wanted those Scrubbers to get out of my way and go home. But they had another idea. All at once they rolled onto their backs to form a moving, shimmering carpet of what looked like flowing black grass.

Ping!

"Zippy says to step on."

Shem cautiously put her right leg onto the quivering field of robotic AstroTurf. Then her left.

"It tickles," she said, standing, vibrating.

"I think I'm going to be sick," Shem's left leg said.

I strapped the Iknatian spear to my back, secured the Birkin, dropped into a forward position and leapt onto the carpet of Scrubbers. In a matter of seconds, a thousand million little legs carried us down the slope, curving around trees and boulders, through dangerous passes and over cliffs. It was like snowboarding on a triple black diamond run, except without a board or snow or helmet.

We came to a stop at the base of the tower, which was as big as a city block. Loretta was waiting for us on the third rung of a spindly ladder that appeared to grow out of the tower's side.

"It's about time," the puffin said.

"We're lucky to be alive," I said, stepping onto the solid, unmoving ground.

Shem laughed and her left leg cursed as they skidded to a stop.

I glanced up. Way up.

The tower rose several miles into the air, narrowing to a single, microscopic point. Which is when it hit me that we had to get to the top of a structure as tall as ten Empire State Buildings stacked one on top of the other. Even worse, the rest of the sky was crowded with too-close planets, stars of all colors and sizes, and spinning galaxies that seemed ready to crash down on us at any moment.

"So we just climb?" I asked Loretta.

The puffin nodded.

"Is there a Command Center up there? One we can get into and talk to somebody?"

"Maybe," she said, shrugging her shoulders.

She was the most unhelpful puffin I'd ever met.

Shem and I scavenged the ground for sprouts, ate a few, and put the rest into my Birkin. Then we waved goodbye to the happy Scrubbers.

"You afraid of heights?" I asked Shem.

"I don't think so," she said.

"I get a little dizzy," Shem's left leg said.

I didn't really care.

"You and Loretta go first," I said.

The puffin soared into the air, heading toward the top of the tower. Shem slung the bag containing her parents' ashes over her shoulder, put on a pair of black leather gloves and started climbing.

The tower was made of squishy red plastic and rubber, and it was covered with long, fibrous strands that looked like thirty- to fifty-foot Twizzlers. Getting to the top was not going to be easy, even for a skilled (and strikingly beautiful) athlete like myself.

I took a deep breath.

I felt the cool air pass through my hair and the holes in my shredded boot.

I climbed.

There's a lot of time for reflection and self-examination when you're climbing to the top of an endless tower on an illegal spaceship while worlds are crashing all around you. But since I knew pretty much everything about myself (all good), I ignored that and instead tried to think about how to save the universe.

There was the poem, of course.

I am here.
I am a broken heart.
I am the cry of a lonely soul.

It was sad, like Shem said. But my two big questions were: "Who was 'I'?" and "Where was 'here'?" If I knew the answer to those, I was certain I'd be able to track down whoever it was, convince them to turn off the black hole, and sit back and have a couple of doughnuts and maybe a drink with a little umbrella. Logically, it made sense that "here" was Eris, since that's where we were. And the sad and sorry "I" was probably the pilot or operator of the spaceship. (I hoped.) If that was the case, he or she just needed to buck up and smile and get a hobby and stop with the whining and crying. (Not to mention turn off the scary black hole ASAP.) I mean, it's one thing to feel sorry for yourself, but to drag everyone else in the universe down with you, that's taking it a bit too far.

"How are you doing?" I shouted.

"Good," Shem said, climbing hand over hand into the unknown.

"This wasn't in my contract," Shem's left leg complained.

My hope was that at the top we'd find a big button that would shut down the death spiral. It didn't seem likely, but there was a lot about the universe I didn't know. (Believe it or not.) I mean, Cardamon Webb talked about repairing entire constellations and upgrading galaxies and fixing the plumbing that went from the Outside and the Other side to the Inside (the sewer of the universe). If all of that was possible, why not a big On/Off switch for a black hole? (It would be too easy, that's why.)

"What's at the top, Alice Jane?" Shem shouted.

"A spectacular view," I said, trying to stay positive.

It was a good question. In my mind, the top of the tower was the "Command Center." But I had no idea what it controlled, if anything. The spaceship, probably. And the scrounging of the universe, perhaps. And the fighting and the killing and the war, possibly. Maybe even the black hole itself. I mean, the Krone told me I'd somehow figure everything out once I got to the top, but to be honest I didn't have much faith in an artificial construct who lived in a place that didn't exist. Know what I mean?

"Alice Jane, this tower is like a big sprout," Shem said, nibbling on the end of one of the long red rubbery strands.

"What's it taste like?" I asked.

"Broccoli," she said. "Yuck."

Shem was a lot easier to travel with than Dodobrain. (Which isn't all that difficult.) I mean, she actually knew important stuff, like how to put together an amazing warrior princess outfit and how to fix a broken Scrubber. And she didn't trip all over herself or gripe about anything. By now Wilkin would've complained about blisters and climbing and mud and Norwegian crusted scabies. Or turned our mission into a reality TV show with a Secret Weapon and a dozen unknown celebrities. Shem just climbed.

"I hope there's a bathtub and a loofah up there," I said.

"And a place for my mom and dad, too," Shem said.

That made me think about Jasper and where he'd end up. In my opinion, a spaceship is a crummy place to leave somebody's ashes. Especially when there are Scrubbers all around that want to clean away dust, dirt, grime and the remains of the dead. Like I've said before, Jasper needed a special place, even if that meant carrying him around in the Birkin for the rest of my life.

"What day is it, Alice Jane?"

"One or two days left," I said.

Calendars didn't matter. Not anymore. Neither did the days of the week. I measured time in terms of the countdown to the End of Everything. It was like heartbeats. How many beats did the universe have left before its heart stopped?

"What happens when we die?" Shem asked.

"We're not going to die," I said.

"But what comes after?"

Another good question. We were more than dust or ashes, I was sure of that. In fact, my long-term plan for the next six months was to become "as one" with the Great Void. I was already more than halfway there. (Probably closer to 95%.) I mean, I knew everything about healing and compassion (duh), and I walked (and climbed!) the path of peace and enlightenment. And there was all the dog poop I'd cleaned up and the tuna noodle hot dish I'd served to the hungry because of my community service hours. Clearly, I was just a few months away from oneness with the universe.

"You okay up there?" I shouted to Shem.

"It's a long way, Alice Jane," Shem shouted back.

We'd been climbing for almost five hours and needed a break. I caught up with Shem and we straddled the rungs and chewed on some sprouts that didn't taste like broccoli. Loretta joined us, happy to relax for a couple of minutes.

As we sat and enjoyed the scenery, the wind grew stronger and more dangerous, and the tower swayed back and forth about six feet in either direction. One misstep or involuntary sneeze and it'd be sayonara and goodbye.

"Um, Alice Jane," Shem said, pointing, "there's somebody coming."

I looked down.

A quarter of a mile below us, a dark shape climbed toward us up the ladder.

23

Dave

"Looks like a regular party," said a voice from the shadows.

Everybody turned and backed away as a brown, mailbox-shaped reptilian creature with gray spots, buggy eyes and sharp teeth stepped into the light. A pink, forked tongue dangled out of its open mouth, quivering.

"That's far enough, mister," Grimes said, raising his axe.

"Make yourselves at home," the creature said, ignoring the Sergeant. "Oh, you already have. Foolish me."

"I think that's a Nevarian Marted Tooey," Digger said under his breath. "Never seen one in real life before, though. Or I don't think I have."

"You are quite right," the creature said, acknowledging Digger. "I am also called The Creature That Dwells in the Depths. You may call me Dave, if you like."

Sal dug into her backpack and retrieved a small guidebook titled *Fauna from Austana to Zewana*.

"Dave," I said with greater confidence than I felt, "I'm Wilkin Delgado. My friends and I are just passing through your very attractive air duct on our way to the Command Center."

"Best to stay away from that place. They're not too welcoming," Dave said. "Not like me."

"Digger," Grimes said, "what's a Nevarian Marted Tooey?"

"It ain't a good thing," Digger said. "Hold onto your brains, everyone."

"According to my guidebook," Sal said, "they live in out-of-the-way solar systems and 'feast on humanoid blood and flesh.' It also says they 'read minds.'" She looked up at Dave and then back at the page in the book. "There's a small photo, but it's not very good. Looks something like Dave here, I suppose. And those zeppelin-sized droppings we noticed in the blast area and scattered around on the floor? Definitely his."

"There is a good deal of misinformation in your little book," Dave said defensively, his tongue darting in and out of his mouth. "For example, we cannot read minds, per se. We more or less read emotions. Feelings. Inklings."

"Baloney," Loaf said.

"Allow me to use you as an example, sir," Dave said to Loaf, pausing for a second. "Behind that lazy and cynical exterior, I see despair and hopelessness and fear. And loneliness, too. It's not easy being you, now, is it? What a poor, sad, pitiful, friendless soul." Dave paused. "Shall I go on?"

Loaf lowered his head and withdrew to a spot next to Philbus Trot, who was hiding behind the eight priests of The Holy Order.

"We just want to get through to the Command Center, that's all," I said. "We're getting ready to leave right now."

"And we don't care about your tricks," Loaf shouted out.

"Oh, but you do, you do," Dave said. "Everybody wants to know secrets."

Philbus Trot cleared his throat.

"Dave, Dave, Dave. No need for threats or hocus-pocus. We mean you no harm," he said, parting the row of priests and stepping forward. "I am Philbus Trot. Former Ambassador and one-time owner of this fine world. You've no doubt heard of me."

"No," Dave said brusquely, shaking his head.

"I say we get out of here," Sal said.

"I agree with Private Salanatwicz," Jot said.

"Thanks for your hospitality and good conversation, Dave," I said politely. "We have to be going."

"What's the hurry?" he said, taking two steps to his right to block our escape. "First we need to get to know each other a little better, don't you think?" He scratched his head thoughtfully. "Let's exchange some juicy secrets, shall we?"

"We're not playing your games," Grimes said.

"I'll start," he said. "One of you is a liar and not what he pretends to be." Dave looked at me. "One of you is homesick and terrified." He pointed a curved black claw at Scuzz, who was squatting on the floor sharpening his sword, oblivious to everything. "One of you is greedy and rapacious and selfish and uncaring." Dave's tongue danced out of his mouth in the direction of Philbus Trot. "One seeks fame and fortune at all costs." He tipped his head in the direction of Jot. "Eight of you are filled with empty, mystical thoughts." The priests began chanting in low voices. "One of you is living in several dimensions, his mind scattered everywhere—quite confusing." He stared at Digger, who wore his normal bewildered look. "One of you is afraid of being found out." He looked at Reggie. "One is oh-so-lonely, and desperately in need of attention." Ozzie's face turned red. "One of you just wants to be noticed and loved." He winked at Sal. "And one of you is filled with frustration and anger and…honor. Quite noble, actually." He gestured toward Grimes. Then Dave surveyed our entire group. "I believe that's everybody. Except me. And I'm easy to read, wouldn't you say?"

He blinked three times and grinned.

"None of that matters," I said. "We're leaving now."

"Oh, but it does matter, Mr. Liar. You see, I like to get to know my meals before…well, before," Dave said. "Feelings do influence the taste. Something like salt and spices."

"You're going to eat us?" Ozzie said fearfully.

"I didn't sign up for this," Reggie said, swallowing hard.

"I have been following your news feeds very closely," Dave said. "There was a chance you would be dropping by. And here you are."

Grimes raised his axe and made a slight move in the direction of the garrulous creature, and then screamed and collapsed onto the floor.

"That was a mistake. You see, I can recognize your feelings in an instant. You wanted to slice me in half with that dangerous weapon of yours," Dave said, kicking Grimes' writhing body. "As you have discovered, my own emotions can inflict a good deal of torment when necessary."

We were in trouble. Big time. (As you probably guessed.) Even though we had that Nevarian Marted Tooey outnumbered eighteen to one, he knew our every feeling and could anticipate our every move even before we did. But what could we do? I did a quick inventory of possible weapons I had on me: My bug pin (no bugs), the Key to the City of the Dead (no locks), the big leather book in my backpack (just words), and a toothbrush and minty-fresh toothpaste (no help). That left my Power Rangers boxers and the duct taped, recycled sword that gave me a shock every time I tried to use it.

I didn't like my chances.

"No, Dave," I said, unsheathing the sword and feeling an uncomfortable jolt of electricity.

He stared at me with his buggy eyes. Then he laughed.

"Be careful, Wilkin," Jot said. And to Reggie she said, "Zoom in. Record everything."

"We're right behind you," Philbus Trot said, stepping behind Ozzie who was behind Loaf who was behind the eight priests.

"You got him where you want him, Chief," Digger said confidently.

"Looking for help from your Secret Weapon, are we? The mighty Wilkin Delgado of Warrensberg, Minnesota? The deadly warrior from the Milky Way galaxy?" Dave said, giving each of us a contemptuous look. "I don't think so. In fact, I rather fancy the taste of Mr. Delgado and his lies for breakfast. What do you say to that?"

"I'm not afraid of you, Dave," I said.

I raised the sword high over my head.

"Of course you are," he said.

"Don't let him scare you, Chief," Digger said.

The chanting of the priests grew louder.

"Oh, and it will be painful. Did I mention that?" Dave said. "Pain is the finest of seasonings."

"I don't want to die," Ozzie said, shaking.

The chanting was almost deafening.

"There's too many of us, Dave," I said, sweat dripping out of all three trillion pores in my body.

"You tire me, Mr. Liar," Dave shouted over the noise. "You and your silly friends."

Dave's sharp claws grabbed hold of my neck. Then he leaned forward and his long, forked tongue sought out my face.

My heart pounded.

133

My sword crackled.

Lightning danced.

I screamed.

And then pale yellow slime oozed across the floor.

I looked down and saw Scuzz's well-sharpened sword buried in the back of the Nevarian Marted Tooey's lifeless body.

24

Listen to Your Leg

Go or stay? That was the question.

If Shem and I continued up the ladder, there was a pretty good chance we'd reach the Command Center ahead of the mysterious climber, after which we could get inside and do what we had to do. (Rescue the cosmos, in case you forgot.) But I didn't like the idea of a possible homicidal maniac (or even a persistent life insurance salesperson) sneaking up behind us and invading my beautilicious space.

"Loretta, you and Shem keep going," I said.

"I want to stay," Shem said stubbornly.

"Too dangerous," her left leg said.

"Listen to your leg," I said. "At least one of us needs to make it to the Command Center."

Reluctantly, Shem began to climb, looking back once or twice to make sure I was still okay. Loretta circled the tower and kept a watchful eye on Shem. Me? I did a weapons inventory: Iknatian spear (check), sword (check), Birkin (check), lethal hands and feet (check). Since there was no good place to hide, and since the tower was swaying wildly from side to side, I wrapped an arm and a leg around one of the ladder's side rails and waited, chewing on a few sprouts to pass the time.

Twenty minutes later I could tell the climber was human and wearing black leather armor.

After three more minutes I was able to make out a couple of steel swords.

A minute after that I spotted the dimple on his chin. And the broken nose.

"That's far enough," I shouted into the howling wind.

Dimple Man looked up.

"You!" he said through his wired-shut jaw. "I have not the time, wench."

"*You* don't have the time?" I said. "Have you looked at the sky lately?"

His eyes darted from one edge of the heavens to the other.

"Witchcraft and sorcery."

Was this the Middle Ages?

"Look, you idiot," I said, "we're being sucked into a black hole and everything will end unless I can get to the top of the tower."

Okay, it did sound a bit crazy. Even to me. But I didn't have time for fancy explanations. I just wanted everyone to get out of my way. Dimple Man, on the other hand, didn't care about any of that. And instead of saying, "Gee, Alice Jane, you're absolutely right, what was I thinking?" he advanced slowly, one rung at a time, ignoring the strong winds, movement of the tower and my all-consuming annoyance with everybody and everything (especially him).

I gripped the Iknatian spear in my right hand and balanced the Birkin in the crook of my left arm, then I crouched low in a (sort of) horse stance. But just as I was getting into my defensive position, a great gust of wind blew me off balance. Dimple Man used that moment to sprint up the ladder—his feet taking the rungs two at a time, his hands sliding up the side rails—launch himself into the air and wrap his fingers around my slim and supple left ankle.

Blerk!

I responded with a quick side-kick, striking Dimple Man solidly in the elbow with my right heel. He released his grip, clawed the air and tumbled a few feet before catching hold of one of the many Twizzler ropes on the side of the tower.

Then we fought.

I jabbed him in the gut with the butt end of the spear. He slammed me head-first into the rubbery tower. I swung the Birkin hard against his damaged jaw. He tried to carve me up with his two swords. Blah, blah, blah. (The usual.) We kicked and punched and jabbed and blocked and grappled. After about four hours, we were a tangle of two bruised and exhausted bodies hardly able to poke each other's eyes out. Finally, Dimple Man charged at me in a last, desperate attack. I stepped aside like a bullfighter on a balance beam, and watched as his momentum carried him into the empty air roughly 10,000 feet above the surface of an unfeeling, unforgiving spaceship.

What to do?

I could have let him drop. That would have been easy. But if you want to know the truth, he was the first person I'd met who could match my strength and skill, and he didn't seem to whine or complain too much, either. Also, I was "that close" to becoming one with the Great Void, and I figured saving somebody's life was maybe all I needed to tip the balance in my favor. (Plus, Dimple Man was super cute and I couldn't exactly remember why we were fighting.)

I calculated the geometry of his fall, slid 500 feet down the ladder and (carefully) tucked the blade end of the Iknatian spear underneath my right armpit. Then I stretched out as far as I dared— one hand on a side rail and the other supporting the spear—and watched as Dimple Man's boots, then knees, then shoulders, then turquoise eyes and then mane of curly blonde hair dropped quickly past me. The fingers on his right hand, however, closed firmly around the offered end of the spear and he came to a sudden stop.

As that killer warrior hung precariously over Eris, I looked into his eyes. They asked a very good question: "Why?"

"I may need your help," I said.

He nodded.

After that, all I had to do was get Dimple Man back onto the ladder, climb the remaining half mile to the Command Center and save the universe. Piece of cake, right?

Nope.

A powerful wind bent the tower to one side, after which the structure whipped back like a two-mile-long fly fishing rod, flinging us high into the air so we almost touched the spiraling, colliding galaxies. The two of us clung to the ends of the spear as we went up, stalled and then began to fall toward the ground, accelerating faster and faster.

I was pretty sure I was going to die. (For real.)

That didn't happen.

Loretta swooped down from above and clamped her orange beak onto the shaft of the spear. Her wings beat frantically. Sweat poured off her feathered forehead. And we paused among the wispy clouds for at least two seconds. But that was all. Loretta opened her beak, gasped for breath, said "Sorry" and watched as we (again) began a 10,000-foot free-fall.

I was *positive* I was going to die.

That didn't happen, either.

Shem and her left leg came swinging around the side of the tower like circus aerialists. The left leg's teeth were clamped down on one of the long red broccoli-flavored ropes, and its little arms and legs were wrapped around Shem's upside down right ankle. Shem stretched out like a trapeze artist and snatched the spear out of the air with both hands (with Dimple Man and yours truly still hanging onto the ends), circled around the tower like a tetherball on a rope and set us gently back onto the ladder.

Alive.

"Thanks," I said, even though I never say "Thanks."

"Whatever," Shem said, smiling.

Enough talk. We climbed.

Tired, hungry, windburned and bruised, the three of us (plus Shem's left leg) plodded up the remaining 2,000 feet of that two-mile ladder. Loretta soared around us, shouting out an occasional encouraging comment—"You're almost there!" and "It could be worse!"—to keep us going. (I could've done without that.) All the while, I couldn't take my eyes off the enormous colorful suns and planets suspended overhead. I felt their gravity tugging us in a thousand different directions. And the light and heat from all the stars was intense. (And me with no Ray Ban sunglasses or Josie Maran Argan Daily Moisture SPF 47 lotion.)

The ladder terminated at a two-foot-by-two-foot hatch in the floor of a tiny vestibule that jutted out from a large, gray, planet-shaped building perched at the top of the tower.

I pushed open the hatch and all of us piled into the cramped entry and sprawled across the floor.

We'd made it.

I looked around.

139

There were four walls, a roof, no windows and a single metal door with a doorknob.

I got up and staggered over to the door.

It was locked. (Of course.)

Then I read a small handwritten sign that said: Use Other Door.

25

The Ascendance of The Healer

Scuzz saved our lives.

In case you forgot, the eighteen of us were trapped inside that underground air duct, powerless to overcome the Nevarian Marted Tooey's mind control tricks. As the monster's claws dug into my neck, my brain felt like it was going to explode. Then... it was over. I was alive and Dave was an unmoving heap on the floor oozing yellow goo.

What happened?

My best guess is that Scuzz's overpowering fear somehow masked his thoughts and emotions. And when the time came to do something, he did what his father said—"Don't think, just act"— and ran his extra-sharp sword through the miserable creature's slimy body.

He was a hero.

After that, seventeen of us stood around, dazed, while Scuzz crawled away on his hands and knees and vomited onto the floor.

"Good work, Private," Grimes said, resting his hand solidly on Scuzz's shoulder.

"Got what it deserved," Loaf said, kicking the smelly corpse.

Scuzz was pale and shaking, and probably in shock, but there was no time for healing or celebration. The universe was dying, and there were only a few hours remaining before all of creation would fit on the tip of a porcupine's quill with room to spare.

"We have to get going," I said, helping the boy to his feet.

Scuzz got up and clumsily put one foot in front of the other.

We walked for miles in silence as I tried to clear my mind of tunnel rats and monsters, and to focus on the poem and how to save everything and everybody. My plan? I had to get to the Command Center and talk to whoever or whatever was in charge (I am come) and then show my love of something (I am an open heart) and blast that black hole to smithereens with a blinding light (I am the light of a thousand suns).

It still needed a little work.

The air duct curved to the right and then began to rise. A short time later we spotted an exit door that led to a flight of stairs and the surface of Eris.

"I believe I have satisfied my part of our agreement, Mr. Delgado," Philbus Trot said.

"We're not there yet," I said.

I climbed the stairs, opened another door, stepped outside and found myself at the base of a massive red tower that grew out of the ground and vanished into an uncomfortably crowded sky. The view was both awe-inspiring and surreal. Stars and planets and satellites and superclusters dangled overhead like a child's mobile.

My first thought? We were dangerously close to EOE. My second thought? It was kind of pretty.

"Okay, Mr. Former Ambassador," Grimes said, "where is this Command Center?"

"All the way up," Philbus Trot said, pointing to the top of the tower. "There's an elevator over there on the side."

Grimes rubbed his chin thoughtfully.

"What do we do now, Sarge?" Sal asked.

"Ride the elevator to the top and take over the Command Center," Grimes said.

Sal, Digger and Loaf nodded their heads and pulled out their swords and axes.

"We're behind you 73.65%, Sarge," Digger said, waving his weapon in the air.

I took hold of Scuzz and gently lowered him to the ground with his back against the tower.

"Stay here with Jot, Reggie, Ozzie and the priests, okay?" I told him.

I think he understood, but I'm not sure. You see, as soon as the word "okay" escaped my lips, about thirty or forty soldiers in black leather armor swarmed out of the bushes and surrounded our unit.

"Drop your weapons," the first soldier said.

I ducked behind the eight priests of The Holy Order and crawled along the side of the tower, staying out of sight.

"I don't really take sides in these matters, so if you'll excuse me," Philbus Trot said, preparing to leave.

"Silence," the second soldier said.

"I don't believe you know who you're talking to," Philbus Trot said indignantly.

"You're the guy who's going to be the first to die unless you keep your mouth shut," the third soldier said. "Am I right?"

Philbus Trot closed his mouth.

"Captain Tagg sent us running all over creation to chase down some troublemaking lady warrior," the first soldier said. He looked

143

at Sal. "That you?"

"I don't know what you're talking about," Sal said.

I crawled farther along the rubbery base of the tower until I came to the elevator door.

I glanced back at my unit.

The Hippos (and the rest) were being prodded with swords and axes by the soldiers. I'd have worried about them, except that's when the wool suit-wearing tunnel rats appeared out of the same bushes and surrounded the soldiers who'd surrounded us.

"Live or die. Your choice," Rat #47 told the outnumbered army.

The soldiers hesitated.

"'Someone has to die in order that the rest of us should value life more,'" Rat #48 said.

"That's Virginia Woolf, in case you didn't know," Rat #49 added.

The soldiers immediately handed over their weapons.

Sal pushed past a couple of the disarmed soldiers and greeted the tunnel rats.

"What are you doing here?" she asked.

"We wanted to make sure you were telling the truth," Rat #50 said. "Then we saw you were in trouble and—after much discussion—decided to help."

Rat #51 scanned the faces of the soldiers dressed in black.

"Who are *they*?" he asked Sal.

"The enemy," she said.

The enemy soldiers looked at each other and then at the rats.

"Who are *you*?" the second soldier asked Rat #52.

"The tunnel rats of Eris," she said.

The third soldier pointed at the Happy Hippos.

"And who are *they*?" he asked.

"Missionaries from the Alice Jane Zelinski Foundation," Rat #53 said.

"Who?" the first soldier said.

"The doughnut lady," Rat #54 said.

I'd reached the elevator door. (Thankfully.)

Of course, that's when the thousand priests (minus eight) of The Holy Order came out of the bushes and surrounded the tunnel rats who had surrounded the soldiers who had surrounded us.

The white-robed boy with painted face and hands stepped forward and stretched out his arms.

"We are come as witness to the New Becoming," he said.

"What's he talking about?" Rat #55 asked.

"He's loony," Loaf said.

"We celebrate this joyous transformation and the ascendance of The Healer," the boy said.

I needed to get out of there.

I pressed the "Up" button next to the elevator.

The doors opened.

I stepped inside and pushed the top button.

The doors closed.

I rose silently into the unknown.

26

Anybody Home?

"Use Other Door"? Seriously?

Obviously the people who put up that little sign didn't plan on a visit from Alice Jane Zelinski, otherwise they would have set out a welcome mat and flowers, and unlocked the blerking door.

"What do we do now, Alice Jane?" Shem asked.

"Try knocking?" Shem's left leg said questioningly.

I pounded on the door and waited at least five seconds.

I was pissed (as you probably guessed), so I took a deep, mindful breath and thought about what my social worker Carol would tell me in times like this: "Violence is not the answer to every problem, Miss Zelinski." Which is a bunch of crap.

"Blerk!" I screamed as I grabbed the knob and ripped the door off its hinges.

It felt good.

After that, the five of us (including Shem's leg) poked our heads through the open doorway. The room was larger than the vestibule, and crowded with mops and brooms and brushes and paints and cleaning supplies. As far as I could tell, it was a janitor's closet or supply room.

We cautiously stepped inside.

The walls, ceiling and floor were all made of some weird alien metal I couldn't even scratch. I took two steps forward and pushed aside a rolling cart and a mop bucket on wheels, and cleared a path to the other side of the room. Then I spit and cursed. Directly in front of me was another closed door: A massive, impenetrable piece of polished gray metal with no lock or handle or knob of any kind.

"We're not getting through that," Shem's left leg said.

"A grim omen indeed," Dimple Man said, tapping the door with the tip of his sword.

Not a lot of positivity, in other words.

"Maybe we just buzz ourselves in," Shem said, pointing to a small panel with a keypad and silver push button mounted next to the door.

Loretta nodded.

I stepped forward and pressed the button.

"Anybody home?" I asked.

Alarms and sirens went off and an electronic voice repeated: "Intruder alert! Intruder alert!"

We got the idea.

"Can you shut that thing off?" I shouted into the panel.

The alarms, sirens and warnings stopped, but my ears kept ringing.

"You have breached the security of the Eris Command and Communications Facility," the panel said.

Tell me something I didn't know.

"That's because we want to get inside," I said to the panel.

"This is a restricted area," the panel said. "No visitors are allowed."

147

"We're not visitors," I said. "We're…guests."

That must have confused the panel, because the response took several seconds.

"Who are you?" the panel said.

"Alice Jane Zelinski," I said.

I thought I heard a digital "Hrmph," but I could have been wrong.

"You're not on the list," the panel said.

"It's 'Zelinski' with a capital 'Z,'" I said. "Write it down and open up."

I didn't like the idea of a 5,000-year-old computer voice telling me what I couldn't do.

"I'm sorry, but no man is authorized to enter this secure facility."

Man?

"I'm a woman," I said.

Didn't that control panel have eyes?

"I meant to say that no *living person* is allowed to enter," the panel said quickly.

"I'm dead," I said. "Look it up."

The panel took a moment to check the obituaries. (Or so I assumed.)

"I'm sorry for your loss, Miss, but no person—alive *or* dead— is allowed beyond this door," the panel said. "No exceptions."

"I'm not a person," I said. "I'm a Limited Liability Corporation." I kicked the door. "Look it up."

That control panel was getting on my nerves.

"Yes, of course," the panel said after (probably) locating me on a list of all the LLCs in the universe. "We have strict rules that prohibit unlawful entry. You can't be too careful these days. I hope you understand."

"Whatever," I said.

"Just a few minor details," the panel continued. "Please enter your User ID and 513-character password. And your mother's maiden name."

"Blerk!" I screamed as I drove the Iknatian spear five feet into the bowels of the control panel.

Sparks flew. Connections sizzled.

"Access granted," the panel said pleasantly. "You may enter, Alice Jane Zelinski LLC, deceased."

"That's more like it," I said, spitting into the depths of the panel and listening to the crackle as the rest of the circuits smoked and fried.

The big door opened wide.

We stepped forward into an open area that looked like a planetarium, with a white hemispheric ceiling and a curved, continuous wall that circled the room. About a thousand TV screens covered every inch of the surface and displayed scenes of war and destruction, tranquil forests and lakes, large hydraulic machines, glowing propulsion systems, spiraling galaxies, grazing animals, complex charts and graphs, indecipherable statistics and more.

After a quick look around, I decided that everything was centered around a silver console in the middle of the room. I went over and searched for a big button or switch that said "Black Hole" or "Off."

No luck.

"Is there somebody I can talk to around here?" I shouted, turning to face every possible direction.

Of course not.

I thought about the Krone's words: "You will know." Well, she was wrong about that. I couldn't locate any controls to stop the black hole. And the universe was ready to self-destruct in a few short hours.

"Look over here, Alice Jane," Shem said. She stood in front of a TV screen showing a bleak, muddy landscape with small, featureless shacks and pitiful-looking animals. "It's…home."

It was a live feed of Shem's store and the murky pond where I'd landed.

"And over here," Shem said, moving a few steps to her right, "there's Ga-da-nor and the Krone."

The Krone turned when Shem said her name, and I was pretty sure that artificial lady looked directly at me.

"Cardamon," Loretta said from the other end of the room, gesturing toward the image of a stone fortress surrounded by twelve heavily-armed guards.

Dimple Man stood in front of a scene of death and destruction on the Field of Blood.

"The war," he said bitterly.

The Command Center appeared to be monitoring everything and everybody on Eris.

"You'd better look at this, Alice Jane," Shem said worriedly.

She pointed to a screen showing an unruly crowd of men and women at the base of the tower who were pushing and shoving an army of leather-clad soldiers. All around them, a thousand white-robed figures jostled with at least a hundred scruffy-looking men and women in two-piece wool suits.

"What's going on?" I said.

"It looks like they all want to get to the elevator," Shem said, pointing at another TV screen.

"Elevator? There's an elevator in this thing?" I screeched, shooting a deadly look in the direction of that miserable puffin.

"Who knew?" Loretta said innocently.

Everybody else, it seemed.

Okay, I was pissed again. (For about the forty-seventh time, in case you're counting.) Over the past twenty-four hours I'd risked my precious (and over-the-top gorgeous) body climbing a rubbery ladder two miles into the deadly skies over Eris. I'd survived hurricane-like winds and the burning rays of scores of spiraling suns. Not to mention nearly being sliced into a thousand pieces and/or almost plummeting to my death. And all that time I could've slept in, eaten a healthful breakfast, pushed a button and made the trip in a minute and a half? Argh!

We watched the elevator doors close below.

I instinctively reached for my Iknatian spear, but it was implanted (and probably charred and mangled) five feet deep into that annoying control panel. So I withdrew my sword and got into my forward stance. Dimple Man and Shem unsheathed their own swords. Loretta menacingly chomped her little beak. And Shem's left leg bared its sharp claws.

We were ready.

The elevator hummed for a minute and then stopped.

We charged across the floor.

As I ran, I raised my weapon high. And when the elevator doors separated, I leapt into the air and swung my sword in a powerful death stroke. But just as I was about to disconnect the person's head from the rest of his body, I stopped.

"Wilkin?" I said.

27

Are We There Yet?

"Alice Jane?"

I'm not sure what I expected to find in the Command Center at the top of the tower on that manufactured planet somewhere on the Flipside of the universe, but Alice Jane Zelinski wasn't it. As soon as the elevator doors opened, I screamed, shouted her name, held up my duct taped sword for protection, closed my eyes and hoped I'd keep on living for another sixty or seventy years. (Maybe more.) After a few long seconds, I opened my left eye a crack, then my right eye.

"Aren't you supposed to be dead?" I asked.

"That's what they tell me," she said, sheathing her weapon.

A young girl with black skin and orange lips came skidding up between us. She wore black leather armor and held a three-foot-long sword in her right hand. When I looked down at her feet, one of them looked back at me.

"That's…him," the girl said. "The Secret Weapon. From TV."

As soon as she said that, a warrior with a bruised and broken face, and two deadly swords, spun around, gave a shout and came charging in my direction.

"Breathe your last, knave!" he bellowed.

I nearly freaked. But as he ran past Alice Jane, she jabbed him with one of her sharp elbows and followed that up with a Kung Fu kick to his rear end, which sent him sliding across the floor and crashing into a monitor that was playing some kind of video game.

"Lay off," Alice Jane said to him. "Wilkin is on our side."

"He is marked for death, wench," the man said, getting to his feet and limping toward me. He had big muscles and dirty blonde hair and blue eyes that looked hunted and crazed. "His blood is mine."

"Can't we work this out?" I asked, backing away.

"I was awarded the kill," he said, getting closer and closer.

"*You're* the Assassin?" I said.

Alice Jane placed herself between the killer and me.

"Look, you two, we have a universe to save," she said. "You can settle this after it's all over—one way or the other."

The man growled like a hungry wolf and gave a slight nod of agreement.

"Friends?" I asked tentatively.

He growled again.

Nope.

"Well?" Alice Jane said, turning to face me. "What have you got?"

"The universe is being sucked into a black hole and we only have like two hours left," I said.

"I know that," she said. "Can you turn it off?"

"No," I said, shaking my head. "You?"

"That's what I'm trying to figure out."

Loretta the puffin flew across the room, landed on top of the console and studied the images on the hundreds of monitors.

"What's with all these TV screens?" I asked.

"They tell us what's happening all over the ship," Alice Jane said.

"Ship?"

"Eris is a spaceship," Alice Jane said. "It's been traveling for like 5,000 years and scavenging for spare change across the cosmos."

Huh.

"Okay, tell me what else you found out," I asked.

"Like you said, there's a big black hole that's eating the universe," she said. "I'm supposed to know how to stop it."

"And?"

"I don't have a clue," Alice Jane said in frustration. "All I have is a sixteen word poem I got from an artificial construct named the Krone."

"Me, too," I said. "Except I got mine from a religious cult called The Holy Order of The Healer. They think I'm The Healer—the real one—which I'm not."

"Anything else?"

"The Doris Supercluster is missing," I said.

"Like I care," Alice Jane said.

"Everybody wants me to end the war," I said.

"Of course they do," she said.

"And Philbus Trot wants some kind of special seeds for guiding us to the tower," I said.

"Trot's here?"

She was not happy to hear that.

As we tried to catch each other up on everything we knew about Eris and saving the universe, Loretta and the girl stared at a TV screen showing a skinny old lady in a pink bathrobe.

"It looks like she wants you over here," the girl said.

"What for?" Alice Jane asked.

"Not you, Alice Jane," the girl said. "Him."

"Me?"

"You're in trouble now," the girl's fuzzy foot said.

"Um, who are you and who or what is that…animal?" I said to the girl.

"I'm Shem and that's my left leg," Shem said.

Things were getting weirder and weirder.

I walked over to where Loretta and Shem stood beside the console, and stared at the TV. An old woman in a fluttery robe on top of a mountain stared back.

"You said she asked for me?" I said.

"She wants you to do something," Shem said.

Loretta rapped on the console with her orange beak and gave an exasperated grunt.

I looked down and noticed a tiny keyhole in the otherwise pristine metal surface. I touched it with a fingertip and then clutched the Key to the City of the Dead. The old woman on the TV mouthed the word "Yes," so I slid the Key into the keyhole and turned my wrist.

There was a click, a sigh and a groan as the spherical roof of the Command Center opened like a spring flower and revealed a spiraling universe preparing to suck us and everything into a single point of unlight.

"Are we there yet?" a voice said.

28

The Countdown

Eris was awake.

Dodobrain put the Key That Opens Everything into a keyhole in the Command Center console, and that was all it took. Wilkin, Shem (and her left leg), Loretta, Dimple Man and I watched the roof open and reveal the silent, congested sky. It was scary-looking. All the planets and moons and galaxies were practically sitting on top of us, and spiraling closer and closer.

"Are we there yet?" Eris asked.

I gulped.

"We need you to turn off the black hole," I said. And I added, "Pronto," because it needed to be done really, really fast.

"What?" Eris asked, yawning (I think).

"Look outside," Wilkin said.

"Hard to see anything with all those stars and planets in the way."

"Duh," I said.

I suppose I should have been a bit more understanding. I mean, the spaceship had been traveling for like five millennia, and from the way it sounded, it'd been running on autopilot for at least a thousand of those years. Eris probably still had sleep crud in its digital eyes and stinky wake-up breath in its forward thrusters. But we were out of time.

"Who are you again?" Eris asked.

"Let me catch you up," I said. "We're all going to die unless you can turn off the black hole in like twenty-seven minutes."

"You sure you got the right spaceship?" Eris asked.

"What Alice Jane means," Wilkin said impatiently, "is there's a really black black hole in what used to be a faraway side of the universe, but it's sucking in everything and everybody. We were sent here to turn it off. And in case you can't tell, we don't have a lot of time left."

Pause.

"I see what you mean," Eris said.

"Well?" I said.

"It's not good news, is it?" Eris said.

"Blerk!" I screamed and ripped the console out of the floor and threw it across the room.

"I don't think that's helping, Alice Jane," Shem said.

Yeah, but it felt good.

"So what you're saying is you can't do anything?" Wilkin asked the spaceship.

"I can set a timer, if you'd like," Eris said.

What?

Half of the screens went black, and six big white numbers (and a couple of colons) appeared—00:21:16—and began a countdown.

Now we knew exactly how much time we had left to live.

29

A Conversation

It was up to Alice Jane and me.

We'd risked everything to get to the Command Center, only to find...nothing. No "Off" switch. No magic bullet. No help. The only thing that spaceship could give us was a timer telling how many minutes and seconds remained until the End of Everything.

"We can do this," I said, sitting down on the floor.

"The answer has to be in that poem," Alice Jane said, sitting across from me.

She opened her pink purse and took out an old-looking piece of paper folded in half. I unzipped my backpack and brought out the big leather book.

"Is that how much time is left?" Shem asked, pointing to the monitors showing 00:19:38 and counting.

"Yep," Alice Jane said.

Shem grabbed her duffel bag and took out a pair of shoeboxes. She opened the boxes and removed two plastic bags full of chalky ashes and set them on the floor. Alice Jane pulled a bag of pinkish ashes from her purse and placed it beside the other two.

"What's all that?" I asked.

"Jasper," Alice Jane said.

"My mom and dad," Shem said.

It must have meant something, but I didn't have time to find out what.

"Can you two hurry it up?" Shem's left leg said.

"Back off, furball," Alice Jane said.

The fuzzy creature quickly retreated into Shem's left pant leg.

"I've read the poem at least a hundred times, Alice Jane," I said. "I still don't know what it means."

"It's a bunch of whining, if you ask me," she said. "All that about the 'broken heart' and the 'cry' and the loneliness. I mean, how is that going to save the universe?"

"What are you talking about?" I said.

"All I'm saying is that the guy needs to cheer up and get his head on straight," she said. "And maybe take a few Kung Fu lessons with Master Woo."

I was confused.

"It's not depressing," I said. "It's about an 'open heart' and 'light' and 'suns.'"

"What are *you* talking about?" she asked.

We looked at each other.

"They're not the same," I said.

"There's *two* poems," Alice Jane said.

That changed everything.

"What's yours say?" I asked, leaning forward.

Alice Jane unfolded the piece of paper and read:

I am here.
I am a broken heart.
I am the cry of a lonely soul.

159

"Like I said: Depressed," Alice Jane said. "What about yours?"

I opened the book, located the page with the poem and read:

I am come.
I am an open heart.
I am the light of a thousand suns.

"It's like they're part of the same poem," I said. "Same number of lines and words."

"But it's all teary-eyed and miserable in the first one and all comforting and hopeful in the second," Alice Jane said.

"It sounds like something bad happened in yours," I said.

"Maybe it has to do with the universe falling apart and someone comes to get it fixed. Like Cardamon Webb. And us."

"Unless it's two people," I said.

"What do you mean?"

"Maybe the one is all lonely and sad and the other is joy and light."

"Or like a conversation," Alice Jane said. "'I am here,' he says, and she says, 'I am come.'"

"I'm not sure it's a man and a woman like that," I said.

"That's not the point," she said. "Then it says, 'I am a broken heart,' and the answer is…."

"'I am an open heart,'" I said. "I think you're right."

"But that still doesn't help us," Alice Jane said.

"You say yours was written right after the crumpling?" I asked.

"And foretold 5,000 years ago, if you can believe that."

"The book says my poem is a prophecy handed down from generation to generation, and one guy even said it was a recipe for some kind of stew," I said.

"More like a problem and solution. Or someone hurting and someone else trying to help," Alice Jane said.

"It's like he—it—suffered a terrible loss," I said.

"And the answer is an open heart…and all those suns," she said.

A thousand suns.

Was it possible?

"The supercluster," I said slowly.

"What?"

"The missing supercluster," I said.

"What are you talking about?"

I sat in the middle of the Command Center and stared at nothing.

"I know this is going to sound crazy, but what if…?" I said as though from far away.

"What if *what*?"

"Can a black hole have feelings, Alice Jane?"

30

Something Wacko This Way Comes

Wilkin Delgado is certifiable. (No surprise there.) Our countdown was at 00:14:53 and dropping, and he was dreaming up some story about planets and stars being alive. (He'd gone wacko on me.)

I looked at Shem and rolled my eyes.

"Listen to what he's saying, Alice Jane," she said.

I looked at Loretta.

She nodded.

I looked at the Krone.

She nodded.

I looked at Dimple Man.

He was cleaning his fingernails with a small knife.

Seriously? Fifteen minutes to live and he's worried about dirty cuticles?

I listened.

"So the universe got all squashed together with the crumpling," Wilkin said, "and then everything uncrumpled and went back to the way it was."

"Except…," I said.

"They weren't together anymore," he said.

"So the black hole and the supercluster *missed* each other?" I said. "Are you talking about 'love'?"

"I don't know, Alice Jane. Physical attraction. Something like gravity, but more selective," Wilkin said. "Call it whatever you want."

"And the black hole got so depressed he's recrumpling the universe to find her and get back together?"

"'I am the cry of a lonely soul,'" Wilkin said. "He's not happy."

"But you said the Doris Supercluster is lost," I said.

"That's what Cardamon Webb told me," he said. "And it's like 3,000 galaxies, and twenty million light years in diameter, so it's hard to miss."

"Then it's hopeless," I said. "If that's what's really happening, the death spiral will keep going unless we can find Doris and get the two back together."

We both glanced at the monitors: 00:11:40.

Shem tugged at my sleeve.

"Alice Jane," she said.

"Not now," I said.

"Somebody's coming," she said.

I'd been so busy trying to figure out how to save the universe, I wasn't paying attention to anything else. And we didn't have time for interruptions or distractions.

The elevator doors opened.

"Uh-oh," Loretta said.

It wasn't just somebody. It was a lot of somebodies.

31

One Thread

I felt like I was standing in the middle of Grand Central Station at rush hour.

Hundreds of men and women streamed through the elevator doors and into the Command Center. Some wore white robes, some black or brown leather armor, some dark gray wool suits and some carried camera equipment and boxes of makeup.

"Wilkin," Jot said, red-faced and angry, "you can't just leave us like that. We're a team."

"I'm trying to save the universe," I said. "I think that's more important."

"Do you have any gum, Chief?" Digger asked.

I shook my head.

"Reggie," Jot said, "set the camera there." She pointed to the spot where the console had been torn away. "Medium close-up on Wilkin. Now."

"Who are all these people?" Alice Jane asked me.

"The Happy Hippos, which is Sergeant Grimes, Digger, Loaf, Scuzz and Sal. And the film crew, which is Jot, Reggie and Ozzie.

And there's the tunnel rats of Eris, The Holy Order of The Healer, and some warriors in black I don't know." Then I pointed to Philbus Trot, who was coming our way. "Him you know."

"An unexpected pleasure, Miss Zelinski," Philbus Trot said, smiling. "You gave us quite a scare thinking you had breathed your last."

"Yeah, I heard about the Foundation, Trot," Alice Jane said.

"Zelinski? The doughnut lady?" Rat #56 said.

"They told us you were dead," Rat #57 said.

"I'm kind of somewhere in between right now," she said.

"'Life and death are one thread, the same line viewed from different sides,'" Rat #58 said.

"Sacred words of Master Lao," Alice Jane said with a prayerful bow.

"That's…right," Rat #59 said. "She's right."

The rats looked at each other and fell silent.

"You the one we're supposed to kill?" one of the soldiers in black asked Alice Jane.

"Probably," she said. "But I'm kind of busy right now. Check back in about ten minutes."

Sergeant Grimes pushed his way through the crowd.

"You track down the person in charge, Delgado?" he asked me. "We need to end the war."

"I'm working on it, Sarge," I said. (Even though I wasn't.)

As everybody talked or plotted or quoted or chanted, Alice Jane, Shem, Loretta, Philbus Trot, the Assassin and I edged away and huddled together near the center of the room.

The countdown was at 00:07:14.

"It's like a party in here," I said.

"Focus, Wilkin. Focus," Alice Jane said. "We need to find that supercluster."

What could I say? She was right.

"Okay, according to Cardamon Webb," I said, "Doris disappeared right after the crumpling stopped. And Eris came through that same area at about the same time."

"So there's probably a connection," Alice Jane said.

"Let's say Eris was scavenging for whatever, and picked up...."

"Three thousand galaxies?" Alice Jane said skeptically.

"Hey, it could happen," I said. And then added an uncertain, "I think."

"The Krone did say Eris compresses things, and catalogs and stores them inside the ship. I'll give you that," Alice Jane said.

"You see?" I said.

"But we're talking twenty million light years across," she said even more skeptically. "That's really, really big."

"It's all I've got, Alice Jane," I said, throwing up my hands.

"So you're saying we ask the ship to release the supercluster—if it's even there—bring the two lovebirds back together and everybody lives happily ever after?" Alice Jane said.

"Do you have a better idea?"

She shook her head.

"Eris!" I shouted. "We need your help."

"What now?" Eris said.

"I'm looking for something you scavenged about a year ago," I said. "The Doris Supercluster."

"And the Seeds of Slebe, if you would," Philbus Trot interjected.

Huh?

"I'll check," Eris said.

"We're running out of time, aren't we?" Shem said.

"I knew this was going to happen," her left leg said.

166

The future looked bleak. We desperately needed some good news—and a little luck.

"My catalog lists both items," Eris said.

Yes!

"Um…can we have them?" I asked.

"Not without the authority of PT Amalgamated Properties LLC," Eris said. "Or the authorization of the estate of Alice Jane Zelinski LLC."

"That's me," Alice Jane said.

"It says here you're dead," Eris said.

"I am."

"And you give your permission?"

"Yes," Alice Jane said. "And hurry up."

A small seed packet appeared in Philbus Trot's right palm.

"The seeds," Eris said.

Philbus Trot quickly slipped the packet into his pocket.

We waited for a minute. Then another.

"What about Doris—I mean, the supercluster?" I asked impatiently.

"Gone," Eris said.

32

Nothingness

"What do you mean 'Gone'?" I asked.

"Absent. Not here," Eris said.

I was getting pissed again. (Big surprise, right?) As you know, things were not going well. We only had a few ticks of the clock left to live, and somehow we had to find the missing Doris Supercluster, which even a lovesick black hole couldn't locate. In situations like this, my social worker Carol would tell me, "Take it one breath at a time, Miss Zelinski." But what do you do when you run out of breaths?

"You can't just lose a supercluster," I said.

"Where did it go?" Wilkin asked.

"I'm not sure," Eris said. "I was playing a game at the time."

"Game?" I asked. "What kind of game?"

"After a couple of thousand years, travel becomes somewhat tedious," Eris said. "So I created a simple war game. It's running on one of the monitors to your right."

I looked at the screen.

Small groups of pixelated armored figures with swords and

axes moved around on a map while little rockets exploded all around them. The spaceship's score was 82,738,416.

"Is that…?" Wilkin said, looking at the screen.

Yep.

"What else can you tell us, Eris?" I asked, deciding to deal with the missing supercluster first and the video game later.

"There was a sizable power surge, everything had to be reset, and when it was all up and running again, the Doris Supercluster was missing," Eris said.

"When was that?" Wilkin asked.

"At the time of the Reversal," Eris said.

"You mean when the crumpling stopped?" I asked.

"Yes."

"You were there, Alice Jane," Shem said.

"We were all there," Philbus Trot said.

"I don't remember much," I said. "I was kind of busy getting electrocuted and carbonized."

"Me, too," Wilkin said.

The timer was at 00:03:17.

"We need to figure this out right now, Wilkin," I said.

"I know, I know," he said, taking two quick breaths. "Doris was here on Eris. We know that, right?"

"And then she got zapped," I said.

"Probably by the same sixty septillion joules of current that got us."

"Maybe she was carbonized, too," I said. "Or vaporized."

"Or…stolen," Wilkin said.

We looked at Philbus Trot.

"Do you know anything about the missing supercluster, Trot?"

"I'm as much in the dark as the two of you," he said. "I came here to help the Secret Weapon shut down a dangerous black hole.

169

That's all."

I didn't trust him.

"If somebody did take Doris," I asked Philbus Trot, "where could they hide her?"

"Using a simple compression algorithm and a sturdy crowbar," he said, "the supercluster could be hidden almost anywhere."

Seriously?

"But who'd want to steal Doris?" Wilkin said.

"A single galaxy contains a wealth of minerals, inhabitable planets and civilizations, Mr. Delgado," Philbus Trot said. "The question is not 'Who would?' but 'Who wouldn't?'"

"Is that why your spaceship was trolling the cosmos, Trot?" I asked.

"It's like fishing, Miss Zelinski," Philbus Trot said. "You set out your nets and see what turns up."

"Like 3,000 galaxies?" I said.

"Perhaps," he said.

I didn't know where to go from there. (Other than get really, really mad, that is.) I mean, according to Philbus Trot, just about everybody in the universe had a motive to steal Doris. Plus, she could be anywhere. And finding that supercluster was the only way to save us all.

In other words, that was it: End of Everything.

As the last few minutes of my precious life ticked away, Dodobrain sat and stared off into nothingness.

And then he turned and stared at me.

It was creepy.

"Alice Jane," he said, "what if we're asking the wrong question?"

"What do you mean?"

"Instead of, 'Where would you hide a supercluster?' what if the question is, 'Where would a supercluster hide?'"

33

A Prayer for Alice Jane Zelinski

I knew.

I looked into Alice Jane Zelinski's fractalized, spinny, swirly face and I knew.

"She's in you, Alice Jane," I said.

"I don't know what you're talking about," she said.

"Doris," I said.

In about two seconds, Alice Jane's expression went from her normal DEFCON 1 level of pissedoffness to utter disbelief.

"You are totally and freakishly demented, Wilkin Delgado," she said.

"I mean it," I said. "Last year when we jump-started the universe, Doris escaped by following the current into your body. That's why you have all those swirly things swimming around inside. It's 3,000 galaxies."

It was the only explanation that made sense. (Even if it was crazy.)

"It fits," Loretta said.

"*Et tu*, puffin?" Alice Jane said, glaring at the bird.

The countdown was at 00:00:43.

"That really black black hole has been looking everywhere for Doris," I said, "but he can't find her because she's locked inside of you." Then I added, "You're the prophecy."

"Are you just saying that because we're all going to die, or do you actually believe that crap?"

"Does it matter?" I asked.

It didn't. And we both knew it.

"Okay, then shut up and tell me what to do," Alice Jane said.

All around us I felt a chilling silence as tunnel rats and soldiers and filmmakers realized that time was running out and all of creation was hanging by a thread between life and death. The Holy Order of The Healer formed a ring around the six of us (plus Shem's left leg) and began to chant.

"This is a little dramatic, don't you think?" Philbus Trot said.

"Shut up, Trot," Alice Jane said.

"I'm scared, Alice Jane," Shem said, rocking back and forth on the ground as she hugged the two bags of white ashes.

"It'll be over soon, Shem," Alice Jane said, squeezing the girl's hand.

Shem's left leg curled into a ball and trembled in fear.

Alice Jane picked up the bag of pink ashes and held it close. "Say a prayer for me, Jasper," she whispered.

Sweat dripped from every square inch of my body as I opened the big leather book. As unbelievable as it sounds, The Holy Order was right: I was The Healer. And it was up to me to save the universe. (I hoped.)

"Repeat these words," I said. Then I drew a breath and read: "'I am come.'"

I expected Alice Jane to be homicidal (or worse), but instead she seemed to be at peace with whatever was going to happen. (At least for the moment.)

"'I am come,'" she repeated.

The chanting continued.

"'I am an open heart,'" I said.

If I got this wrong, everything was screwed. And if I was right…Alice Jane Zelinski was going to kill me.

"'I am an open heart,'" she repeated.

The chanting grew louder. At the same time, the Command Center began to shake and the entire spaceship began to wobble. All around us cracks appeared in the walls. Equipment sparked and smoked. And every part of my body felt like it was being pulled apart.

"'I am the light of a thousand suns,'" I said.

It was the answer to the black hole's cry of pain and loss. A call…and then a response. And a reunion.

Maybe.

"'I am the light of a thousand suns,'" she said.

The universe paused.

"Nothing's happening, Wilkin," Alice Jane said.

"That's because I have to do something," I said.

The countdown was at 00:00:11.

"What are you waiting for?" she said. "There's like ten seconds left before the universe is squashed to the size of a blackhead. Don't wimp out on me, Dodobrain."

"You're not going to like this, Alice Jane."

"Right now I don't care what I'm not going to like," she said. "We're out of time."

What did Scuzz say? "Don't think. Do it."

I tore the Key to the City of the Dead from my neck.

I gripped it tightly in my right hand.

Then I plunged the Key through Alice Jane's leather armor and chain mail shirt, and deep into her heart.

I was right.

She didn't like it at all.

34

Fireworks

My body exploded.

Planets and satellites and galaxies spewed out of my chest and into the swirling spiraling skies above. I was like a cannon shooting a column of glittery light into the cosmos as star after star escaped to fill the voids of emptiness and loneliness.

Barely conscious, I glanced at one of the TV screens. The countdown had stopped at 00:00:00 and I could vaguely hear the beep-beep-beep of an alarm.

The first thing I thought was somebody needed to turn off the blerking timer. (It was giving me a headache.) The second thing I thought was we'd reunited the Doris Supercluster with the black hole and saved everything and everybody. (Hooray!) The third thing I thought was this was the biggest fireworks display I'd ever seen and I had the best seat in the house. (Also hooray!) The fourth thing I thought was that my body was being ripped apart and I was in unimaginable pain and the chances of my surviving something like this were zero or less. (Upside down smile.) The fifth thing I thought was I'd come all this way to give Jasper a proper burial and ended up needing one of my own. (Ironic, don't you think?)

Wilkin had figured it out: I was the prophecy.

"I am come," it said. And I came. "I am an open heart," it said. And my heart was opened. "I am the light of a thousand suns," it said. And the starlight from within me was set free to heal a terrible loneliness.

At the end I remember seeing white and pink sparkles carried away by the cosmic winds.

And my world became blackness.

Om Ami Dewa Hri.

35

Stardust

I watched her die.

At the exact moment I stabbed Alice Jane in the heart with the Key to the City of the Dead, stars and planets came shooting out of her body like a Roman candle on steroids, disappearing through the open roof and into the vast, unspiraling cosmos beyond.

"No!" Shem cried out as she sobbed and clutched Alice Jane's stilled hand.

"I had to," I said.

Shem knelt tearfully beside Alice Jane for the longest time, and then opened the three bags of ashes. She tossed the remains into the streaming, burning light that was 3,000 galaxies, and watched as the particles vanished in bursts of white and pink splendor, and were carried off to their own special place in the universe.

"They're stardust, Alice Jane," Shem said through her tears. "My mom and dad. And Jasper."

"Let's not get too weepy-eyed, people," Philbus Trot said, covering his nose and mouth with a PT-monogrammed silk handkerchief. "After all, the rest of us are still in one piece."

"Shut up, Trot," Loretta said.

Minutes passed. Maybe hours.

As the last of the "thousand suns" escaped from Alice Jane Zelinski's body, the Assassin leaned down and closed the tug-o-war champion's eyelids with a callused fingertip.

"A valiant warrior," he said. "May she find peace in the next world."

"The other side of the thread," Rat #60 said.

"It was the only way," I said to anybody, nobody, myself.

Alice Jane was gone—for real, this time.

That's when I remembered something else.

"The war. I think I can stop it, Sergeant Grimes," I said.

"Do what you need to do, Private," he said. "That's why we're here."

"Eris," I cried out, "stop the fighting!"

"How can I help you?" Eris asked.

"You've been playing that video game for thousands of years," I said, "but it's not a game, it's real."

Sal turned to Loaf.

"What's he talking about?" she asked.

"Stupid games," he said.

I stared at the TV screen with its display of animated war, destruction and death.

"You're killing people, Eris," I said. "Millions of them."

"Games can't kill," Eris said.

"This one can," I said. "You're giving people axes and swords, ordering them into battle and then shooting them with real rockets. To you it's a game." I stopped and then started up again. "More than eighty million men and women are already dead. That's how you're keeping score. Shut it down."

Pause.

"I…didn't realize," Eris said.

The screen showing the video game froze and the monitor went dead.

"That's it?" Sergeant Grimes said grimly. "We've been fighting for nothing?"

"It's just like a real war," Digger said, "because it is."

I was exhausted. I'd done all I could. The black hole and Doris were reunited. The universe was saved. The war was ended. And everything was in balance again.

Almost.

Above us, the skies cleared and a single speck of pink stardust drifted down from the heavens and through the uncovered roof. It lazily circled Alice Jane's steaming body, paused like a silent prayer, and continued its descent until it came to rest deep within her open heart. Then her skin glowed an electrifying shade of pink and the terrible wound in her chest closed without seam or scar.

"Just a bit of space dust, everyone," Philbus Trot said, flicking a few stray flakes of dandruff from his shoulders. "Nothing to worry about."

But it was more than that.

Alice Jane's eyes flashed open and she dragged a jagged breath into her lungs.

"Blerk!" she screamed.

Alice Jane Zelinski was back.

36

A Crossroads

"Ouch," I said.

I was conscious. (Almost.) I had the biggest headache in the universe. (Duh.) My internal organs were flipping and flopping and out of step like a bad sixth grade marching band. (Not good.) And my incredible drop-dead gorgeous supermodel body was 99.99% clear of all intergalactic residue. (I was pretty sure.)

"You're alive," Shem said, joyfully wiping tears from her eyes.

"Give me a few minutes and I'll let you know," I said.

I rubbed my pounding head and looked around. I was in the Command Center. Shem, Wilkin, Loretta, Philbus Trot and Dimple Man were all staring down at me. And the people in white robes, dress suits, and black and brown armor shuffled around in a daze like they didn't know what to do with themselves.

"Alice Jane, Alice Jane, you should have seen it," Shem said breathlessly. "Everything was going to end and then Wilkin stabbed you with that key and your body spit out all those galaxies and we didn't blow up or crumple to death or anything and then mom and dad and Jasper became stardust and Jasper came back and made you alive and then you woke up and it's right now. Can you believe it?"

"What?" I said.

"I'm really sorry, Alice Jane," Wilkin said. "I couldn't think of a good way to explain what I had to do."

"You mean tell me you were going to stab me in the heart with that blerking key? I would have killed you first."

"That's what I mean," Wilkin said.

I blinked hard a couple of times.

"Miss Zelinski," Philbus Trot said, pushing through the crowd. "Quite the theatrics. Who would have suspected you of concealing an entire supercluster? Who would have expected you to rise from the dead for a second time? You're full of surprises."

"You're full of something," I said.

Philbus Trot checked his pocket watch.

"As enjoyable as this is, I must be on my way," he said.

"Where are you going?" Wilkin asked.

"Unfortunately, the Foundation will need to be put in mothballs for the time being," he said. "Miss Zelinski's current condition is—how shall I put it?—inconvenient for the cause."

"Sorry for living, Trot," I said.

"Other possibilities have opened up, however," he said, touching the pocket of his suit coat and smiling.

"So what's with the seeds?" I asked.

"A small price to pay for rescuing you and Mr. Delgado—and saving the universe—don't you think?"

He was going to take credit for everything. Just like before.

What a weasel.

"Are they magic beans or something?" Wilkin asked.

"The Seeds of Slebe can grow almost anything. A galaxy.

An army. A fortune." He glanced at Shem. "A new appendage, perhaps." He smiled. "The Seeds are one of the three Great Secrets of the Cosmos." He paused. "Four, if you count me."

I nearly barfed.

As Trot droned on about how the Seeds had been lost for generations and accidentally picked up by the wandering spaceship, Shem's left leg crawled stealthily around the feet of hundreds of priests of The Holy Order, approached Philbus Trot from behind, stood on its fuzzy tiptoes, slipped its head into the former Ambassador's pocket, emerged with the packet of Seeds between its teeth and scurried over to where Shem sat on the ground.

"What's this for?" Shem said.

The leg mumbled something, but it was hard to tell what because of the package between its teeth.

"Time for me to skedaddle, boys and girls," Philbus Trot said. He strolled to the elevator, pressed the button, stepped inside, turned to face us, adjusted his necktie and disappeared.

I got to my feet.

"What do we do now?" Rat #61 asked.

"Go back home, I suppose," Scuzz said.

"Our path is as yet unknown," the boy-priest of The Holy Order said.

That gave me an idea.

"Shem," I said, "get Zippy up here."

I turned to address everyone in the room.

"Listen up," I shouted. "Two miles below us there's about a million Scrubbers that need a coat of paint, a few racing stripes and their own Twitter accounts. So if you have some free time"—like a couple of decades—"they'd appreciate your help. Any takers?"

The Holy Order chanted their agreement.

"We'd be serving humanitarian interests throughout the cosmos like your Foundation," Rat #62 said eagerly.

"Yeah, what the hell," Loaf said.

I went into the supply closet, pushed aside some cleaning carts and a case of gray duct tape, and discovered cans and cans of paint stacked to the ceiling, along with about half a million paintbrushes.

As The Holy Order of The Healer, the tunnel rats of Eris and the out-of-work soldiers from both armies carried the paint and brushes into the Command Center, Dimple Man approached Wilkin and me.

"My time here is at an end," he said.

"So you're not going to kill me?" Wilkin said.

It was the first I'd seen Dimple Man smile.

"Delgado," he said, "I am humbled by your courage."

Courage?

"He almost killed me, you know," I said.

Dimple Man turned to face me.

"Our paths will cross again…wench," he said, and then he laughed, sprinted across the floor, through the storage room, and down the two-mile ladder. (FYI: I got his cell phone number and email address first, though.)

"Alice Jane," Wilkin said, "I have to go, too."

"We're still stuck on this stupid spaceship, in case you forgot," I said.

"Hey, Digger," Wilkin shouted across the room, "can you take me back to Earth in that Flipper of yours? There's a case of Fanta in it for you."

"Strawberry?"

"Naturally," Wilkin said.

"You're a light at the end of the drugstore, Chief," Digger said.

I guess that was a "Yes."

"What about you, Alice Jane?" Wilkin asked me.

Good question.

Did I want to own the universe again? Manage a bazillion corporations and businesses? Buy all the shoes and handbags I could dream of? Spread gift shops and doughnuts throughout the cosmos? Create a new line of high-fashion Zelinski-branded leather armor in pink? Or did I want to become one with the Great Void.

I was at a crossroads.

I looked up into the night sky where everything seemed so small and far apart. What held it all together? It wasn't dark matter or elementary particles or anything like that. It was friendship and love.

I was living proof.

"Jasper," I whispered to the stars, "thanks for saving my life again." Then I searched the vast dark spaces of the cosmos. "And Doris and your black hole friend, I hope you'll be happy for eternity."

I felt a tug on my belt.

"Here, Alice Jane," Shem said, handing me the Seeds of Slebe. "These are yours."

"You take them," I said. "Trot said they can grow anything." My eyes traveled down to the girl's missing limb.

Shem looked at her left leg.

Her left leg looked back.

"I don't need fixing, Alice Jane," she said. "I'm perfect just the way I am."

"You got that right," her left leg said.

I had to agree.

www.ingramcontent.com/pod-product-compliance
Lightning Source LLC
Chambersburg PA
CBHW070029120726
47909CB00003B/1105